Beowulf

In Modern English Verse

British Museum MS. Cotton Vitellius A. xv, fol. 147r (ll. 782–804)
(By permission of the British Library)

In Modern English Verse

Translated and Annotated by

Sung-Il Lee

With a Foreword by

Robert D. Stevick

CASCADE *Books* • Eugene, Oregon

BEOWULF IN MODERN ENGLISH VERSE
Translated and Annotated

Cascade Books
An Imprint of Wipf and Stock Publishers
199 W. 8th Ave., Suite 3
Eugene, OR 97401

www.wipfandstock.com

PAPERBACK ISBN: 979-8-3852-7631-8
HARDCOVER ISBN: 979-8-3852-7632-5
EBOOK ISBN: 979-8-3852-7633-2

Cataloguing-in-Publication data:

Names: Lee, Sung-Il [translator]. | Stevick, Robert D. (Robert David), 1928– [foreword writer]

Title: Beowulf in modern English verse : translated and annotated / Sung-Il Lee, with a foreword by Robert D. Stevick.

Description: Eugene, OR: Cascade Books, 2026 | Includes bibliographical references.

Identifiers: ISBN 979-8-3852-7631-8 (paperback) | ISBN 979-8-3852-7632-5 (hardcover) | ISBN 979-8-3852-7633-2 (ebook)

Subjects: LCSH: Beowulf. | Monsters—Poetry. | Dragons—Poetry. | English poetry—Old English, ca. 450–1100. | Grendel (Monster)—Poetry. | Epic poetry, English (Old)—History and criticism.

Classification: PR1585 L36 2026 (print) | PR1585 (ebook)

Manufactured in the U.S.A. MARCH 13, 2026

In memory of
My father and mother

Contents

Foreword

Why read this translation of *Beowulf*? Because there isn't a better one to be found. Here are the reasons I say this:

It reads so well aloud. The text did so in its oldest form, and it must do so in any translation worth reading. This translation from Old English is oral composition, first heard, and then written down to be heard again. Nothing gets in the way of oral performance of an account of heroic actions, in heroic times, shaped and tempered by wisdom of the world and reflections upon the upshot of human endeavors. It is that performance that is the poem, and it is that which the translation manages so well to give us anew, in Modern English verse.

Nothing gets in the way. The commonest impediments to successful translation have been theories of this and that, High Principles to be upheld, or just romantic notions about "olde tyme" English poetry. Sometimes it is a choice to imitate the general sound of the original text—two half-lines separated by syntax but linked by alliteration. The one successful instance came many, many years ago from Charles W. Kennedy, but even this text tends to accelerate unfittingly as the rhythm continues unrelenting. Sometimes it is a decision to imitate the blank verse of the Renaissance. Sometimes it may be choice of a verse-form such as nine-syllable lines defended by reasoning rather than readability. Sung-Il Lee's translation is not trammeled in any ways like these. The syllable-count is unpredictable: it is instead the phrasings that embody the verse rhythms.

It is not merely the metrical basis of the translation that has to be right. The syntax must be right at the same time. This means simply: the flow of phrase by phrase within the clauses and sentences must move steadily and never stumble, never create a tangle that a reader has to pause and undo. Such is hard enough to manage under any circumstances, but it is often neglected—or despaired of—in translating Old English verse, chiefly because of the prominence of "variation," "the very soul of the Old English poetical style," as Frederick Klaeber expressed it. When a sentence-part gets re-expressed, and sometimes re-expressed again, and sometimes yet again, a sentence may move haltingly once it leaves the metrics of Old English style: "I wish to announce to the son of Halfdane, the glorious prince, my business here, to thy lord" (344–46a) is a piecemeal translation patterned on the original text. Translating verse-by-verse, half-line-by-half-line when possible, can't keep the sentences going aright in Modern English. Sung-Il Lee's resolution of these problems is successful consistently: the variations are not discarded, but re-folded into patterns that keep the text moving forward. Typically at least one of them is delayed—just as the *Beowulf*-poet always does—so that with its occurrence the syntax requires a hearer to loop back (mentally) to the syntactic slot of a prior variant, to a tacit experience yet again of the accumulated syntactic structure. It's a marvelous device for regulating the pace of the narrative, the reading, the telling, to keep it ruminative rather than fit only for a pell-mell tale of adventure and monster bashing.

There is something similar, though it is actually an innovation, in the repetition of a small sentence part, after a delay, which triggers reflective replay of the related portion of a sentence. It, too, controls the pace of the poem. In 930–31 it is simply "may," or in 2158–59 "had"; in 2124–25 it is merely "could not."

Also regarding pace and continuity—cohesion, in fact—of the mix of a "main" narrative, reflections, "episodes," and "digressions": in reading this translation I had a sense of the sweep and cohesion of the source text that I have not found in other translations. The way in which the section divisions come and go is also impressive (and incidentally highlights the independence of section divisions from "natural" divisions of the poem). Similarly, in local passages, say, 1292–1311, the pace is never compromised as the topics shift here and there within the large memory that the whole poem embodies.

The meter and the syntax—the flow of sounds and the flow of sentence-parts—can be right, and there is still the matter of the words we hear, in the translation. Imitation of the original text by trying to mimic it is a temptation to many, but always leads to inferior translations. Without an exception a compound noun or adjective in the original text is right and powerful, but enigmatic or awkward if rendered piecemeal in the lexicon of Modern English. Here is where a translator's tact—not theory—has to be active, and his word-sense entirely in tune with the poetic texture. Unferth is going to challenge the hero in front of everyone; he *onband beadu-rūne* (501), which says he "unbound" his "battle-rune," according to glossing conventions, obscure enough that Klaeber paraphrases it as "commenced fight." Lee's rendering: he spoke, "Revealing his revulsion." A group of warriors who *hrēa-wīc hēoldon* (1214), "held a place of corpses" in the basic glossary reading, reads "Kept the place filled with bodies," conveying the sense exactly without the opacity of glossary-transplants. At 2999–3000 there is a stack of compounds in variation which would be grotesque in word-by-word translation; so we get "That is the malevolence and the mutual malice, / The deadly hate between men . . . ." The most affective word choice perhaps is one of the simplest and most obvious: "the old (one)"—for *þām gomelan* (2817) and *se gomela* (2851)—is accurate, but empty of both force and feeling. When it is read out as "the old man" (and not just once) for Beowulf in his defeat and death from his fight with and defeat of the fire-dragon, it is evocative of the grief of Beowulf's lifelong companions, and of the listeners to this poem: "The old man."

These right renderings of the text are found at every turn: *heortan wylmas* (2507) becomes "his pulsating heart"; *līce gelenge* (2732) makes good sense as "with fleshly legacy"; *mæl-gesceafta* (2737) is caught just right with "the dictum of destiny." A notoriously dense and complex passage of kennings and variations describing the funeral-fire for the hero is rendered faithfully and most effectively this way:

> Wood-smoke arose,
> Black over the fire; the roaring flame bellowed,
> Mingling with the weeping—the twirling wind died out—
> Till it had burnt down the bone-wrapping body-flesh,
> Hot in its heart. With their souls soaked in sadness,
> They mourned the death of their lord, deep in their hearts.
> (3144b–3149)

The choice of words is always true to the text being translated, and always belongs to the active literary language of Modern English. There just aren't any convenient calques, bland approximations, or mere glossary insertions. From the past four-hundred years of language of literature in English it draws extensively, but without any sign (or smell) of "olde tyme" diction. The words are chosen from a heritage of current English. And each one seems (and smells) like a careful choice by a connoisseur of English literary composition. Any number of times I reached for my Modern English dictionaries, both British and American, to check on the semantic range and the etymology of various words in the translation, and never found a flaw with an unexpected choice: "turbid" for *gedrēfed* (1417), for example, or "woven link by link by hand" for *hondum gebrōden* (1443), or "palanquin" for *bær* (3105).

Having said these things about the ways of translating, a brief observation should be made about the competence of the translator. Any translator must face choices among the possible meanings of any part of the source text, in light of the debates and arguments among scholars and, ultimately, his own sense of the text itself. (Never mind that two of the very popular "translations" in the past forty-some years were versifications of translations done initially by others.) It is clear that Dr. Lee has read extensively in the editorial discussions, and his text shows a successful series of choices among the ambiguities and cruces, let alone the obscurities of the original text of *Beowulf*—the blow-by-blow action of the Beowulf-Grendel wrestling match (745–61), for example; or the theft from the dragon's hoard (2216–31).

Forty-five years since I began leading others through the labyrinth of diction, variation, narrative embellishments of *Beowulf*, and reading their translation examinations, and reading most of the published translations; and forty years since I began scrutiny of the spellings and graphotactics system of the sole manuscript text. When I carefully read this new translation line by line, making notes on the many surprising but always interesting locutions, the movement forward was felt all the way through, with even the episodes and digressions (as they are usually regarded) seeming to be at first unproblematic, and then appearing, as they should, as beautiful assets to the action-narrative and its affectivity. In brief, the translation by Dr. Sung-Il Lee succeeded better for an old reader (that I am) than earlier ones have done, and my sense is that it will succeed very well for readers with any degree of less familiarity with the earliest known text. If we still offered seminars on The Art of Translation, this would be a good centerpiece. An old poem here, unimpaired in translation. It is the best we have among the remnants of Anglo-Saxon culture, and in its newer voice.

Robert D. Stevick
University of Washington

Prefatory Note

This volume is meant to serve dual purposes: sharing with the general readers—who may not have been exposed to the old language in which *Beowulf* was composed—the pleasure I have had over the years while reading it, *and* providing the serious students of English language and literature with a translation for them to refer to while they tackle the Old English text.

My memory goes back to my youthful days when I struggled with Frederick Klaeber's *Beowulf* text for the first time, verifying what I could gather from looking up word after word in his Glossary, by referring to E. Talbot Donaldson's prose translation and Edwin Morgan's verse translation. It was an excruciatingly arduous journey of groping over an apparently never-ending misty path. Yet each time I found what I had managed to construe with the help of Klaeber's Glossary to concur with Donaldson's translation or Morgan's, the joy was compensation enough for my toil, which then seemed almost Sisyphean. I hope this volume will turn out, for the students of Old English, comparable to what the translations by Donaldson and Morgan were to me in my youthful days.

No less weighty is the sense of mission I feel toward myself as well as the students of Old English and the general readers. Providing a Modern English verse translation of *Beowulf* that can touch the heartstrings of the readers has ever been a dream of mine. Not for a vainglorious motive. English is an acquired language to me; and I have been a student of English language and literature all my life. Walking out onto the stage to show all I have come to claim as my own is a scary occasion that will tell whether my lifelong dedication has been a worthwhile one. If my lines can please the ears of the English-speaking people and receive an approving nod of the *Beowulf*-scholars, I shall be happy.

Any of the authoritative texts, edited by such scholars as Frederick Klaeber, Elliott Van Kirk Dobbie, and A. J. Wyatt (later revised by R. W. Chambers), can be chosen to be the anchor for translating the epic. But I did not stick to any of the three editions of the *Beowulf* text. Whenever I found any textual discrepancy between them, I turned to Julius Zupitza's transliteration of the Cotton Vitellius Manuscript, in hopes of arriving at a reading that would strike the right note for me as a translator. I must confess that my reading of the original poem, insofar as the textual variants are concerned, has been eclectic.

The sole extant manuscript of the poem bears Roman numerals indicating the allocation of *fitts*. Although Elliott Van Kirk Dobbie eliminated these Roman numerals in his edition, I restored them in the text of the original poem as well as in my translation.

My modern English translation of *Beowulf* was contained in *Beowulf in Parallel Texts* published by Cascade Books in 2017. On this occasion of publishing a volume containing only my Modern English translation, my gratitude to the late Professor Robert D. Stevick—a lifelong *Beowulf*-scholar, who read my translation carefully and decided to enrich my dual-language edition with his foreword—is renewed. The late Professors Derek Pearsall and Gregory Rabassa, I believe, will allow me to have their observations on my work printed again for this volume. My heartfelt gratitude to the late Professor J. Harold Ellens is renewed for his strong moral support on my project, and having recommended my work to Cascade Books. I am grateful to Professor John M. Hill, who has given moral support for my work, while extending friendship with me over the years. Finally, I wish to thank Dr. Robin Parry, who provided a number of helpful suggestions in the final stage of editing *Beowulf in Parallel Texts*, and Emily Callihan for her effort to make this book compatible with the readers.

Introduction

Reading *Beowulf* aloud always proves a unique experience: it allows the reader to relive the moments of listening to a minstrel's recitation of the epic and participating in the poetic situation of oral delivery and aural reception. The lapse of ten centuries since the time when the poem was composed and recited is no hindrance to our reliving the moments of the mutual transaction between the vocal performer and the auditor. This realization consolidates our belief that the *Beowulf*-poet must have envisioned the "theatricality" of the poetic situation that the lines he was composing would create while being recited—an awareness of the poem in the making. Every single line reflects the poet's keen awareness of the impact that its sound quality will have on the auditors' imagination. Narration at any given moment thus mandated the poet's full exertion of his verbal power for a maximum effect of striking the right notes in conveying the poetic messages.

The major task of a translator of the poem is thus to make the sound quality of the original lines felt all along in translation—to transfigure it in a modern tongue all the way through. In order to attain that goal, neither providing a word-to-word lexical rendition nor creating new verse for the sake of comfortable reading in a modern tongue will do. Within the confinement set by the verbal rhythm and the sound quality of the original poem, a translator must produce verses acceptable to the ears of the speakers of a modern tongue.

Here are some of the principles that I have tentatively set up in translating *Beowulf*:

i. Since the original text is heavily loaded with alliteration, the translation should reflect its sound quality by containing as much alliteration as possible;

ii. The verse rhythm maintained in the original text, each verse containing on-verse and off-verse, should be reflected in the translation with verses containing *caesurae*;

iii. The translation should be in a colloquial language with idiomatic expressions; it should be in a *live* language—easy to follow, both in aural perception and oral delivery;

iv. The translation should evoke the sense of remoteness both in time and place, but it should be attained through the use of familiar language;

v. The word order and the sentence structure in the original text should be honored; but the text of a translation should sound natural. In other words, the original lines should reverberate in the translation.

Rather than prolonging a discussion on the theory and practice in the translation of *Beowulf* with critical jargon, I will go directly to what I have done, sampling a few passages in my translation, in hopes of having the readers' reception of them attuned to mine.

Beowulf's first adventure is, of course, his encounter with Grendel. The appearance of Grendel in Heorot after Beowulf's arrival at the Danish court, therefore, has to be narrated with a lot of dramatic tension, for it is the first encounter with the monster—not only for the hero of the epic, but for the audience or the reader:

Com on wanre niht
scriðan sceadugenga.   Sceotend swæfon,
þa þæt hornreced   healdan scoldon,
ealle buton anum.   Þæt wæs yldum cuþ,
þæt hie ne moste,   þa Metod nolde,
se scynscaþa under   sceadu bregdan;—
ac he wæccende   wraþum on andan
bad bolgenmod   beadwa geþinges.
Ða com of more   under misthleoþum

Grendel gongan,   Godes yrre bær;
mynte se manscaða   manna cynnes
sumne besyrwan   in sele þam hean.
Wod under wolcnum   to þæs þe he winreced,
goldsele gumena   gearwost wisse
fættum fahne.   Ne wæs þæt forma sið,
þæt he Hroþgares   ham gesohte;
næfre he on aldordagum   ær ne siþðan
heardran hæle,   healðegnas fand!
Com þa to recede   rinc siðian
dreamum bedæled.   Duru sona onarn
fyrbendum fæst,   syþðan he hire folmum æthran;
onbræd þa bealohydig,   ða he gebolgen wæs,
recedes muþan.   Raþe æfter þon
on fagne flor   feond treddode,
eode yrremod;   him of eagum stod
ligge gelicost   leoht unfæger.
Geseah he in recede   rinca manige,
swefan sibbegedriht   samod ætgædere,
magorinca heap.   Þa his mod ahlog;
mynte þæt he gedælde,   ær þon dæg cwome,
atol aglæca   anra gehwylces
lif wið lice,   þa him alumpen wæs
wistfylle wen.   (ll. 702b–34a)

It is a cliché that there should be correspondence between sound and sense in poetic lines. This principle of poetic composition is fully actualized in the above passage. Apart from the fact that the lines are heavily charged with alliteration, there is a certain sound quality that we can hardly miss. The resonance of the lingering sound [om], [un], and [um], for instance, helps to build up a certain atmosphere of ominous eeriness. The repeated use of the sibilant [s], along with the [sh] sound—

scriðan sceadugenga. Sceotend swæfon, (line 703);
se scynscaþa under sceadu bregdan;— (line 707);
mynte se manscaða manna cynnes
sumne besyrwan in sele þam hean. (ll. 712–13)—

creates the illusion of hearing the sound of serpentine gliding, or of sensing the gradual approach of foggy mist, though we cannot clearly envision Grendel with any definite physical shape. The gradual approach of the monster to Heorot, his tearing the door open in fury, stepping onto the hall floor, and casting his eyes glaringly on the thanes fast asleep—all this is narrated in one sweep of breath in the couple of dozen lines (ll. 710–34a) quoted above. My effort to make my translation reflect what I read in the above passage has led me to the following rendition:

Striding in the dark night,
The shadowy stroller came. The warriors were sleeping—
Those who should guard the gabled building—
All of them, except one. It was well known to men
That, when the Lord willed it not, the devilish foe
May not draw them beneath the dark shadows.
But watching out for the wretch in wrath,
He waited for the outcome of the fight in fury.
Then from the moor under the misty slopes came
Grendel, gradually approaching, bearing God's ire.
The direful destroyer of mankind intended
To take one in his grip in that lofty dwelling.
He advanced beneath the clouds to the wine-hall,
Till he most clearly discerned the golden hall
Gleaming with gold plates. Nor was it the first time
For him to seek the home of Hrothgar.
Never in his days of life, neither before nor since,
He found the hall-thanes a harder lot to bear.

Then to the hall the marauder made his way,
A stranger to life's joy. The door sprang open,
When his hands gripped the fast-forged bar.
He pulled it open to break the hall-door,
Wrapped up in anger. Then quickly
On the flowery floor the fiend stepped,
And walked in, full of anger. In his eyes
Gleamed a flame shooting out an ugly beam.
He saw in the hall many a man of strength,
A band of kinsmen, sleeping together,
A troop of young retainers. Then he exulted
At the thought of tearing, before dawn broke,
Each one's life from his body, as the horrid fiend
Intended, his mouth watering in anticipation
Of a lavish feast.

One of the most chilling and startling passages in *Beowulf* appears when Hrothgar depicts the marshland where Grendel and his mother dwell. In retaliation for Beowulf's physical victory in his first encounter with Grendel, the defeated monster's mother makes an assault on Heorot, and Æschere becomes a victim of her vengeful attack of Hrothgar's palace. Grief-stricken by the loss of his beloved thane, Hrothgar asks Beowulf to venture to visit the underwater dwelling of Grendel and his mother in order to eliminate the root of all the evil that has devastated his land.

Hie dygel lond
warigeað wulfhleoþu, windige næssas,
frecne fengelad, ðær fyrgenstream
under næssa genipu niþer gewiteð,
flod under foldan. Nis þæt feor heonon
milgemearces, þæt se mere standeð;
ofer þæm hongiað hrinde bearwas,

wudu wyrtum fæst   wæter oferhelmað.
Þær mæg nihta gehwæm   niðwundor seon,
fyr on flode.   Nō þæs frod leofað
gumena bearna,   þæt þone grund wite.
Ðeah þe hæðstapa   hundum geswenced,
heorot hornum trum   holtwudu sece,
feorran geflymed,   ær he feorh seleð,
aldor on ofre,   ær he in wille,
hafelan [hydan];   nis þæt heoru stow!
Þonon yðgeblond   up astigeð
won to wolcnum,   þonne wind styreþ
lað gewidru,   oð þæt lyft drysmaþ,
roderas reotað. (ll. 1357b–76a)

Hrothgar's description of the moorland where Grendel and his mother dwell is a chilling narration that makes any reader of *Beowulf* shudder: the dreadful landscape that the lines invoke is unmatched by any passage that has ever been written to depict a nightmarish scene the human imagination is capable of envisioning. Here is my Modern English rendition of the above passage:

They inhabit a hidden land—
Wolf-infested slopes, windy headlands, and
A perilous fen-path, where the mountain-stream
Falls down in the mist from the headlands
And flows beneath the earth. Not far from here,
A few miles away, stands the mere,
Over which droop trees covered with frost.
The wood darkens the water with entangled roots.
There every night a fearful wonder is seen—
Fire flaring on the water. None alive among men,
No matter how wise, knows how deep it is.

Fleeing from far off, chased by hounds, a stag
May seek a holt-wood to hide his strong horns;
Yet he will rather give up his life, lingering
On the bank, than plunge his head into the pool
To save his life; that is not a pleasant place!
From there surging waves rise up,
Darkening the clouds, while the wind swirls,
Threatening storms, till the air turns choking
And the sky howls.

Any student of Old English poetry will face the exhilarating and painful moment of reading the last passage of *Beowulf*. The excruciatingly arduous journey is about to reach its end; and the memory of turning the leaves of the glossary provided by that literary giant, Fr. Klaeber, is about to recede into the past. It is a moment of tremendous relief—entailing a sense of wistfulness and regret over not having to cope with the lines—not for some time, at least. The *Beowulf*-poet must have felt the same way, as he was reaching the end of his epic, the composition of which must have exhausted him, both emotionally and physically. All this is reflected in the lines that conclude the epic. Beowulf, our hero, is no more; and those who have survived him, whether his thanes, or the listeners of the heroic saga, must mourn the passing of the warrior-king into the realm of the remote past and oblivion.

Þa ymbe hlæw riodan   hildedeore,
æþelinga bearn,   ealra twelfe,
woldon care cwiðan,   [ond] kyning mænan,
wordgyd wrecan   ond ymb wer sprecan;
eahtodan eorlscipe   ond his ellenweorc
duguðum demdon,—   swa hit gedefe bið,
þæt mon his winedryhten   wordum herge,
ferhðum frēoge,   þonne he forð scile
of lichaman   læded weorðan.

Swa begnornodon   Geata leode
hlafordes hryre,   heorðgeneatas;
cwædon þæt he wære   wyruldcyninga
manna mildust   ond monðwærust,
leodum liðost   ond lofgeornost. (ll. 3169–82)

When a student of literature encounters lines like these, he or she should feel that the notes one could ever hope to hear at the end of a work have finally hit the eardrums. Here we find the convergence of what we have wished to hear and what we hear—the complete fusion of what the text has been brewing in our hearts and what we finally have attained after reading so many lines! It is a moment of catharsis; and the lines of *Beowulf* are finally loosening their grip on our heartstrings:

Then the battle-brave ones rode round the mound—
Inheritors of noble blood, twelve all told—
Uttering words of grief over loss of their lord
In a mournful dirge to commemorate their king.
They lauded his manliness, and spoke highly of
His brave deeds—as it befits a man
To praise his dear lord in words,
While longing springs in his heart, when he
Is finally freed from the confinement of flesh.
So the people of Geatland mourned the death
Of their lord, recalling the warmth of his hearth.
They said that, of all earthly kings, he was
The gentlest of men, the most warm-hearted,
Kindest to his people, and most eager for fame.

When I was reading the very last passage of *Beowulf,* the above was roughly what I heard in my mind's ear. I would not call it a translation; the above is only an echo of what dug into my heart while I was reading the concluding lines of the epic. Though falling short of the emotional elevation attained by the lines in the original text, the above was the outcome of my desperate attempt to revive in a modern tongue the most magnificent passage literature has ever produced.

Poetry means condensation of verbal expressions of human thoughts and emotions; and it demands not only succinctness but also accuracy in hitting the right notes that capture all the feelings that have to be expressed. When the *Beowulf*-poet wrote that the Geatish warriors had built a monument holding the ashes of their lord on a promontory, so that the sailors could see it from afar, it was an indirect way of expressing the poet's wish that his work would be read and remembered by his posterity for a long time. Here is the convergence of what the actual lines of a poem say and what the creator of the work really wanted to say. As the last lines of the epic fade away with the last twang of the minstrel's harp, both our hero of the epic *Beowulf* and the poet who composed the more-than-three-thousand lines recede into the past—along with the fading out of the minstrel's voice. The last couplet contains a series of superlatives:

> manna mildust ond monðwærust,
> leodum liðost ond lofgeornost. (ll. 3181–82)

The emphatic use of the superlatives notwithstanding, the repeatedly heard sound [st] somehow leaves the lingering note of wistfulness over the poem that has reached its end. The epic opened with the powerful and fully inflated ejaculation, "Hwæt!" Now the very last lines create the feeling that the air is being released from an inflated ball. With the four adjectives in the superlative, carrying with them the tired minstrel's hoarse voice, the poet himself steps back into the past, as does the hero of the epic.

Translation means reliving the moments when the poet was composing the lines. It is not a later-age person's attempt to record what he or she has understood while reading the original lines for the readers. As a translator's pen glides on a blank sheet, it should be a moment that resurrects the agony that the poet embraced, while groping for the right words, line after line.

Beowulf

[1–52: Scyld Scefing, a foundling, grows up to become a mighty ruler of the Danes, and dies in old age, leaving his son Beow behind to succeed him.]

What! We have heard of the glory
Of the Spear-Danes' kings in olden days—
How those princes performed deeds of valor.
    Not a few times Scyld Scefing seized
The seats of banquet from many a tribe,
Mighty opponents, and terrified the earls.
Since the time when he was found a deserted infant,
He grew up in tender care, soared to the sky,
And prospered with unparalleled honor, till
All neighboring nations over the sea came
To obey and pay tribute to him: a good king he was!
To him a son was born later—a toddler
In his large dwelling, whom God sent
To comfort the nation. He saw the dire distress
Of those who had long suffered without a lord
To rule them; in that cause, the Lord of life,
The Ruler of glory granted him worldly honor.
Beow[1] attained renown—his name spread wide—
The son of Scyld, all over the land of the Danes.
Such is what a young man, while in his father's protection,
Must do, through manly acts and bounteous bestowing,
To secure the blessing in old age of having
Close kinsmen and loyal subjects to stay near
In times of war; of whatever clan, a man

1. Here and in line 53 the name "Beowulf" appears in the manuscript; so does it in Klaeber's and Dobbie's editions. In this translation, however, I used the name "Beow" in referring to Scyld's son, to avoid confusion with Beowulf the Geat, the hero of the epic. Scholars explain the appearance of the name "Beowulf" at this early stage of the poem as the consequence of scribal mistake.

Is bound to prosper through praiseworthy deeds.
Then at his destined hour Scyld the strongman departed,
Embarking on a journey to the bosom of the Lord.
Then his dear followers carried him to where
The waves surge, as he himself had bidden,
When the lord of the Danes ruled with his words.
He had kept them long as their dear lord.
There at the harbor stood the ring-prowed ship,
The prince's vessel, covered with ice and ready to set out.
Then they laid down their dear lord,
Their renowned ring-giver, in the bosom of the ship,
Right by the mast. Many a treasure had been
Brought there, precious things from faraway places.
I have not heard of a ship more grandly adorned
With weapons and battle-gear,
With bills and coats of mail; on his breast lay
Many a treasure, which was bound to go
Far with him, drifting on the powerful waves.
They no less lavishly provided him with gifts,
People's treasures, than those who did
At the outset let him float down alone
As a child, drifting on the turbulent waves.
To boot, they set up a golden banner for him,
High over his head, let the sea bear it,
Gave it to the ocean; for them sadness welled in hearts,
Grief overflowed the hearts' brim. Men cannot
Tell truly—hall-thanes or field-warriors—
Who received the cargo beneath the sky.

[53–85: Prosperous reign is carried down to Hrothgar, Beow's grandson, who decides to build a banquet hall, which he later names Heorot.]

(I) Then in the castle Beow of the Danes, dear
Prince of the people, long remained renowned
Among nations—his father and lord having gone elsewhere,
Away from his earthly dwelling—till for them again
Rose high Healfdene, who, aged and fierce in battle,
Ruled the glorious Danes while he lived.
To him four children all told were born
In the world, to the leader of the bands:
Heorogar and Hrothgar and good Halga;
I have heard that . . . was Onela's queen,
Dear bed-sharer of the Heatho-Scilfing.[2]
Then to Hrothgar was granted success in battles,
Warlike glory, so that his friendly kinsmen obeyed him
With all their hearts—till the youth grew to command
A great band of retainers. It came into his mind
That he would give out the order that men build
A pavilion, the greatest mead-hall that
The sons of men had ever heard of,
And therein distribute to the young and the old
All the possession that God had given him—
Except public property and people's lives.
Then, I have heard, it was widely bidden
That many a clan throughout the world
Partake in building the folk-stead. It came to pass in time,
Forthwith among men, that it became quite ready,
The greatest of halls. He named it Heorot,

2. Heatho-Scilfing ("War-Scilfing") refers to Onela, king of the Swedes, son of Ongentheow.

He who had the power to make his words widely listened to.
He did not fail to keep his promise to dispense rings,
Treasure at feast; the hall towered,
High and wide-gabled: it waited for the hostile flames
Of a dreadful fire; it was by no means time yet
That hostility between a son-in-law and his father-in-law
Came to rise after a deadly feud.[3]

[86–193: Grendel, a monster dwelling in the moorland, makes an assault on Heorot, and devastates the Danish court.]

Then the powerful demon could hardly endure
Distress—he who dwelt in darkness—
That he heard loud merrymaking every day,
Coming from the hall; there was the sound of a harp,
The minstrel's ringing song. He who could unfold
The origin of mankind from far back, asserted
That the Almighty created the earth,
The beautiful plain surrounded by streams,
Established the triumphant sun and moon,
The luminaries to lighten the land-dwellers,
And adorned the regions of the earth
With branches and leaves, and also created life
For each of the races, which move about alive.
Thus the retainers lived in mirth,

3. The eventual destruction of Heorot in fire mentioned here has no relevance to the events covered in the poem. However, allusion to the feud between Ingeld the Heatho-Bard—husband of Freawaru, Hrothgar's daughter—and Hrothgar, which led to the burning down of the mead-hall, seems to denote the futility of all human aspirations and attainments—a unifying theme of Old English poetry. Beowulf, upon returning to his homeland after defeating Grendel at Heorot, mentions the role Freawaru would play as a possible peacemaker by getting married to Ingeld, in his report to Hygelac (ll. 2020–69).

Happily, till a certain fiend of hell
Began to perpetrate an act of atrocity.
The grim demon was called Grendel,
A notorious borderland haunter, he who held the moors
As fen and stronghold. The unhappy creature
Warded the region of the race of monsters awhile,
Since the Creator had him condemned
As Cain's kin—then the Eternal Lord
Punished the killing, in which he slew Abel.
Cain did not rejoice at the feud, but the Lord banished him far;
The Lord, for the crime, drove him away from mankind.
From him arose all the evil brood,
Giants and elves and evil spirits—
The very giants who contended against God
For a long time; the Lord gave them proper requital for that.
(II) Then Grendel departed to seek out, when night came,
The tall house—to see how the Ring-Danes
Had settled in it after their beer drinking.
Then he found therein a band of retainers
Fast asleep after a banquet. They did not know sorrow,
What men could suffer from; the unhallowed creature,
Grim and greedy, was more than ready,
Fierce and furious, and from their resting place took
Thirty thanes; thence he departed to go
Back to his home, exulting in his booty—
Content with his fill of slaughter, toward his abode.

Then at dawn with the break of day
Grendel's strength was manifest to men.
Following a feast, weeping rose up,
A great cry in the morning; the renowned lord,

The good prince, sat joyless;
The mighty monarch suffered sorrow for the thanes,
When they beheld the track of the hateful one,
The evil monster; that ordeal was too strong,
Loathsome and long lasting! It was not long after,
But on the very next night again he perpetrated
A greater grisly deed, feeling no remorse for it,
A hostile and wicked crime; he was intent on them.
Then many a one sought resting place
Elsewhere at more distance for himself,
Bed among outbuildings, when the hostility of
The one who had ransacked the hall was shown to him,
Made clear by manifest token; he who had fled from the fiend
Remained farther away, and more secure afterwards.
So he held sway and strove against right,
One against all, till the best of houses
Came to stand empty. It lasted for a great while.
The friendly lord of the Danes suffered affliction
For the length of twelve winters, every woe,
Great sorrow. Therefore, it became well known
To men, to the offspring of human kind,
Through sadly sung tales, that Grendel had fought
Against Hrothgar for long, borne fierce hatred,
Perpetrated much crime and atrocity for many a year,
Continual conflict: he would not have peace
With anyone of the Danish host of men,
Remove his deadly evil, or settle with riches.
Nor there any wise man had good cause to expect
Slackening of the sore from the slayer's hands;
But the fiend, the dark shadow of death, was

Relentless in his grip of the old and the young,
Hovered near and ambushed. In darkness he held
The misty moors; men do not know
Where the hellish demons move along, gliding.
In this way the enemy of mankind, the horrid monster,
Often committed a great mass of wicked crimes,
Severe injuries: he inhabited Heorot,
The richly decorated hall, in the dark nights;
He was never allowed to approach the gift-seat,
Treasure for God, nor did he know His love.
That was a great distress to the lord of the Danes,
Battering of spirit: many powerful often sat down
For consultation; they deliberated on the solution,
What would be the best that the brave ones
Could do to rid themselves of the awful horrors:
Now and again they promised sacrifices
At heathen temples, and entreated with words
To the soul-slayer[4] to bring about remedy
And rid them of distress. (Such was their practice,
Hope of the heathens; they thought of hell
In their mind; they did not know God,
The Judge of men's doings, nor knew they God the Lord,
Nor indeed they knew how to praise the Protector of heavens,
The Lord of glory; woe is to him who must
Through dangerous hostility push a soul
Into the bosom of fire, not hope for solace,
Nor change at all! Blessed is he who may

4. The "soul-slayer" refers to the devil, the antithesis of God. It is ironic that the Danes offered sacrifices at heathen temples, rather than at Christian churches, to be rid of Grendel, a descendant of Cain. The emphasis here is that the Danes were pagans, whose souls were not yet redeemed by belief in God. It is, however, an interesting anachronism that, throughout the poem, Hrothgar's words are filled with Christian thoughts.

After the death-day seek the Lord
And ask for peace in the Father's bosom!)
(III) And so Healfdene's son continually brooded over
The care of the time; no wise man could remove
The misery; the hardship that had come upon the people
Was too harsh, loathsome, and long lasting.
It was a grim, dire distress, and the greatest nightmare.

[194–319: Beowulf the Geat makes a voyage from his homeland to rescue the Danes; upon his arrival he encounters a Danish coast guard, who leads the band to Heorot.]

A thane of Hygelac, brave among the Geats,
Then heard at home of Grendel's deeds.
He was the strongest in might of all men
In that time of this life, noble and mighty.
He ordered that a strong ship
Be built for him; he said that he would seek
The war-king, the famous prince, over the sea,
Now that for him there was need of men.
The prudent men did not find fault with
The adventure, though he was dear to them.
They urged the valiant one, studied omens.
He had the warriors chosen from the courageous
Men of the Geats, those he could find
Most brave. He sought the ship with
Fourteen others. The man skilled in seafaring
Showed them how to reach the shore.
In due time the boat was on the waves,
Floating under a promontory. The ready warriors

Went up to the prow; the currents swirled,
Water against the sand; the men bore
Into the bosom of the boat bright weapons,
Splendid armors. The men pushed the ship forward,
The tight-braced vessel ready for desired journey.
Then over the sea, impelled by the wind,
The foamy-necked ship launched most like a bird,
Till after due time on the second day
The ship with a curved prow had made advance,
So that the seafarers could see the land,
The gleaming sea-cliff, the steep hills,
Large headlands. The sea had been traversed;
The voyage was over. Thence up quickly
The people of Geatland stepped onto the land,
And moored the ship. The mail-coats rattled,
The warlike dresses. They thanked God
For their voyage made smooth and easy by His grace.
Then from the wall saw the Danish sentinel—
He whose charge was to guard the sea-cliff—
The bright bosses of shields borne on the gangway,
Ready war-gear; he was gripped by a desire to learn
What on earth these men were, in his thoughts.
Then the thane of Hrothgar rode his horse
Down to the shore, brandishing a mighty spear
Forcefully in both hands, and asked in formal words:
"What sort of fighting men are you,
Protected by coats of mail, who thus have come,
Bringing a tall ship over the watery road,
Hither crossing the waves? What, while I have been
A coast-guard, holding watch by the sea,

None hostile to the Danish people could
Inflict any injury on this soil with a ship-army.
No shield-bearers undertook to come here
More openly, nor have you acquired
Word of leave from my commanders,
Consent of my kinsmen. Never have I seen one,
Among men on earth, mightier than one of you—
Yon man wearing war-gear. That is not a mere retainer,
Bedecked with weapons, unless his appearance belies him—
A peerless sight! Now I must have full knowledge
Of your origin before you go any farther hence,
Deceitful observers on the land of the Danes,
Not one step further. Now you far-dwellers,
Seafaring men, hear and learn my
One-fold thought. It is best to be in a hurry
To make clear whence you are coming."
(IV) The chief answered him, the leader
Of the band, unlocking a hoard of words:
"We are men of the Geatish stock,
And Hygelac's hearth-companions;
My father was well known to the peoples,
A noble chieftain, whose name was Ecgtheow.
He lived through many winters before he went away,
An ancient man, from his dwelling: every wise man
Well remembers him, far and wide throughout the world.
We have come to seek Healfdene's son, your lord,
The protector of people, with well-disposed intention;
Be good to us with words of your counsel!
We have a grand mission to fulfill for the renowned
Lord of the Danes; there shall not be anything

Hidden, of which I think. You know—if it is
Indeed so as we have heard—that with the Danes
A ravager, of what sort I do not know,
An unknown evil-doer in the dark nights,
Manifests in a terrible manner strange hostility,
Injury, and slaughter; about this I can offer
Advice to Hrothgar in all good intention
On how he, wise and good, can overcome the fiend,
If reversal, relief from the distress of the afflictions,
Should ever come for him again,
And the boiling of care may become cooler;
Or ever after he will have to endure tribulation
And distress, so long as stands there
On the lofty place even the best of all halls."

The watchman spoke, seated on his horse,
A dauntless officer: "A sharp shield-bearer
Shall be a judge of each of the two,
Words and deeds, if he can think well.
I hear that this is a band of men well-disposed
To the lord of the Danes. Go forth, bearing
Your arms and armors. I will lead you;
Also I will order my young retainers to guard
Your ship against any of the enemies—
Your fresh-tarred boat on the shore—
Upon their honor, till again it will bear
Over the sea-streams its dear man—
The ship with a curved prow—to the land of the Geats.
Be it granted to such of those acting bravely
That he pass through a battle-storm, unharmed."

Then they set out. The ship stayed still;

The wide-floored ship remained attached to a rope,
Fastened on anchor. The boar-figures shone
Over the cheek-guards decorated with gold,
Glittering and fire-hardened: the warlike emblem held
Guard over life for the grim fighters. Men hastened,
Marched together, till they could see
A timbered hall stately and gold-adorned.
That was the hall most renowned under the sky
Among earth-dwellers, in which the mighty one dwelled;
Its beam shone over many a land.
Then the battle-brave one pointed out for them
The bright dwelling of the brave, so that they might
Go straight to it. A worthy warrior as he was,
He turned his horse, and spoke thus:
"Time for me to turn back. The Almighty Father
May guard you with His favors,
Safe in your ventures! I will to the sea,
And return to my task of guarding against any foes."

[320–490: Beowulf and his band arrive at Heorot; Wulfgar reports Beowulf's arrival to Hrothgar, who orders Wulfgar to admit Beowulf to the royal presence; Beowulf makes a pledge to Hrothgar that he will defeat Grendel; Hrothgar gives a welcoming address to Beowulf.]

(V) The road was paved with stones, the path led
The men marching together. The mail-coats glittered,
Tightly linked by hand; the bright chain-mail
Clanged in the armors, as they first approached
The hall in their fearsome battle-gear.
Sea-weary, they set down their broad shields,

The strong shield-bosses against the wall;
Then they sat on benches. Their mail-coats rang,
The warriors' battle-wear did. Spears stood,
The seamen's arms put together—
The ash-spears gray from above: the armed troop
Was worthy of their weapons. Then a proud warrior there
Asked the men-at-arms about their lineage:
"Wherefrom do you bring your ornamented shields,
Gray mail-shirts and masked helmets,
And so many spears? I am Hrothgar's
Messenger and officer. I have not yet seen
A band of foreign men looking more warlike.
I think that you have sought Hrothgar
For a daring and high purpose, not in exile."

Then to him answered the brave strong man,
The proud Weather-Geat spoke the words,
Hardy under his helmet: "We are Hygelac's
Table-sharers; Beowulf is my name.
I wish to tell the son of Healfdene
My mission to the renowned prince,
Your lord, if he will grant us
That we be allowed to greet his good grace."

Wulfgar spoke, a man of the Wendlas,[5]
Whose spirit was well known to many—
A man of valor and wisdom—: "I will ask on this
The friend of the Danes, Lord of the Scyldings,
Our ring-giver, our renowned prince,
As you have requested, about your undertaking,
And speedily make the answer known to you,

5. Wulfgar is an official at Hrothgar's court; the Wendlas (or Wendle) are inhabitants of Vendel in Uppland, Sweden, or inhabitants of Vendill in North Jutland.

That the good man thinks fit to give me."
He then quickly went to where Hrothgar sat,
Old and gray-haired, with his retinue of earls;
The bold man stepped to stand before the shoulders
Of the lord of the Danes; he knew the retainers' custom.
Wulfgar spoke to his friendly lord:
"Here are brought, coming from afar
Over the expanse of the sea, the people of Geatland;
The men-at-arms call their chieftain
Beowulf. They are in earnest petition
That they might with you, my Prince,
Exchange words. Do not refuse to grant their wish
In your answer, gracious Hrothgar;
Judged from their battle-gear, they appear worthy
Of the esteem of warriors; indeed, their leader is strong,
He, who has led the fighting men here."
(VI) Hrothgar spoke, the protector of the Scyldings:
"I knew him when he was a youngster;
His deceased father's name was Ecgtheow,
To whom Hrethel of the Geats gave for home
His only daughter;[6] his son is now
Pressingly come here, has sought a glad friend.
Then I have heard that the seafarers say—
Those who carried gifts of the Geats
There for their pleasure—that he has
Strength of thirty men in his hand-grip,
Brave in battle. Him God the Holy
Has sent to bestow His grace upon us,

6. Hrethel's daughter married Ecgtheow and gave birth to Beowulf, which means that Hygelac, the third son of Hrethel and monarch of the Geats, is Beowulf's maternal uncle, as well as his liege-lord.

To the West-Danes, as I do hope,
Against the terror of Grendel. I must
Offer him treasures for his brave daring.
Be you in haste, bid them to come in
To see my band of kinsmen together;
Tell them also clearly that they are welcome
To the Danish people."
[Then to the door went
The well-known man,] told the message from within:
"My dread lord, victorious ever, Chieftain of the East-Danes,
Has commanded me to tell you that he knows your lineage,
And you are welcome here to him,
Having bravely sailed over the surging waves.
Now you may go in your battle-shirts,
Wearing your helmets, to meet Hrothgar;
Let your battle-shields wait out here,
The wooden lances also, for the outcome of the talk."
Then rose up the strong man, many a warrior around him,
The band of mighty thanes; some remained there,
Kept guard over the battle-gear, as their chief bade them to.
They hastened together as the man led
Under the roof of Heorot; [the warrior went,]
Resolute under his helmet, so that he reached the hearth.
Beowulf spoke—on him shone his armor,
The mail-coat a smith wrought with all his skills—:
"All hail, Hrothgar! I am Hygelac's
Kinsman and retainer. I have undertaken in youth
Many a worthwhile task. The issue of Grendel
Has come to be known to me in my homeland;
Seafaring men say that this hall, the grandest

Of buildings, stands idle and useless
For every warrior, once the evening-light
Becomes hidden under the heaven's vault.
Then my people advised me,
The best of them, the wisest men,
That I should visit you, Prince Hrothgar,
For they knew what strength I have;
They saw when I from battles returned,
All bloody from my foes, where I had bound five,
Destroyed the giants' clan, and on the waves slain
Water-fiends of night, endured dire distress,
Avenged the pain of the Geats—they had sought trouble—
Crushed the enemies; and now with Grendel,
With the fierce demon, I alone shall have encounter,
Confront this fiend. Now I wish,
Lord of the Bright-Danes, Protector of the Scyldings,
Guard for fighting men, generous friend of good folks,
To entreat you not to deny me one boon—
Now that I have come thus from afar—
That I alone, [and] the band of my troopers,
This pack of hardy men, may be allowed to cleanse Heorot.
I have also heard that the fiend,
For his unwariness, scorns use of weapons.
I take it lightly—so my lord Hygelac
May be pleased with me in his mind—
That I bear a sword, or a broad shield—
That brown stuff—to battle, but with my grip I shall have
A grueling duel with the fiend and give or take life,
As foes hateful to each other; there he who will be
In death's grip shall trust the verdict of the Lord.

I expect that, if he is allowed to attain victory,
In the battle-hall he will, undeterred by fear,
Gorge himself on the Geats, as he has often done,
The choicest of men; there won't be any need
For you to bury me, for he will have me,
All besmeared in blood, if death takes me.
He will bear my bloody body, thinking to taste it,
And the lone one who goes away will eat ravenously,
Staining his moor-stead; no longer will you need
Worry about taking care of my body.
Send to Hygelac, if the battle seizes me,
The best of battle-gear that guards my breast,
The peerless garb that Hrethel once wore,
The work of Weland.[7] Fate always goes as it must!"
(VII) Hrothgar spoke, Protector of the Scyldings:
"For what's been done in the past and for the favors,
You have sought us, Beowulf, my friend.
Your father incurred the worst feud with fighting:
He happened to slay Heatholaf with his own hands
Among the Wylfings;[8] then the clan of the Geats
Could not keep him, for he was a threat to peace.
From there he sought the folk of the South-Danes—
The Honor-Scyldings—over the swelling sea-waves,
When I had begun to rule the Danish people,
And in youth held a wide kingdom,[9]

7. Weland is the blacksmith of the Norse gods. The name appears also in the opening line of *Deor* and in the second line of the fragmentary poem *Waldere*.

8. Heatholaf was a man of the Wylfings whom Ecgtheow slew; the Wylfings were a Germanic tribe.

9. "ginne rīce," (Klaeber); "ginne rice," (Dobbie); "gimme-rīce" (Wyatt and Chambers). The reading by Klaeber and Dobbie means: "a spacious kingdom." The reading by Wyatt and Chambers means: "gem-rich," or "rich in jewels." What to choose is up to the reader.

A strong fortress of warriors: Heorogar, Healfdene's son,
My elder kinsman, was then dead,
No longer alive; he was a man better than I.
Since then I settled the feud with money:
I sent to the Wylfings, over the surge of the waves,
Old treasures; he[10] swore oaths to me.
Sorrow swells in my soul to say
To anyone what Grendel has brought about—
Humiliations in Heorot and sudden assaults—
With his hostility; my hall-troop,
My daring band has dwindled; doom has swept them
Away into Grendel's horror. God may with ease
Deter the devilish ravager from his deeds.
Full often my valiant fighters have vowed
Over ale-cups, drunk with beer,
That they in the mead-hall would remain to meet
The assault of Grendel with grim-edged swords;
Then in the morning when daylight shone forth,
This drinking hall had become drenched all over,
All the bench-boards bedewed with blood,
A hall for horrible gore; I had less men loyal to me,
My dear daring men, for death had taken them.
Sit down now for a banquet, and untie your thoughts
And the past triumphs to men, as your heart urges."

[491–668: A banquet is held at Heorot to welcome Beowulf; Unferth speaks to disparage Beowulf's martial prowess; Beowulf retorts to Unferth; merriment is renewed and Beowulf gives a pledge of triumph to Wealhtheow; the banquet is over and Hrothgar retires to bed.]

10. "he" refers to Ecgtheow, whose feud with the Wylfings Hrothgar settled by paying them *wergild*.

Then for the men of the Geats to sit together
A bench was cleared in the beer-hall.
There the strong-willed men went to sit,
Sure of their strength. A thane tended the task,
Who bore in his hands an embellished cup for beer,
Let them share shining bubbles; a minstrel sang meanwhile,
To be heard in Heorot. There was mirth for the men,
Not a small band of the Danes and the Weather-Geats.
(VIII) Unferth spoke, son of Ecglaf,
Who sat near the feet of the lord of the Scyldings,
Revealing his revulsion—for him the plan of Beowulf,
A daring seafarer, was cause enough for displeasure,
Because he would not allow that any other man
Should ever dare attain more glory on earth
Than he himself under the heavens would:
"Are you that Beowulf, the one who contended with Breca,[11]
Competed in swimming across the wide waves?
There you two for vanity ventured the depths,
And for your dotard-like boast in the deep water
Risked your lives; no one, friend or foe,
Could keep the two of you from
Plunging into peril, when you dared into the deep.
There you two covered the sea-current in your arms,
Waded through the waves, hastened your hands,
Slid over the surge; the sea swelled with waves,
Winter's welling. You two in water's domain
Seven nights strove. He who overpowered in swimming
Was the one with more strength. Then in the morning

11. Breca was the chief of the Brondings.

The sea bore him up where the Heatho-Ræmas[12] live;
From there he sought his sweet homeland,
Dear to his people, the land of the Brondings,[13]
The fair fortress where he had his folk,
Town, and treasures. All vow made against you
The son of Beanstan[14] faithfully fulfilled.
Then I expect an outcome worse for you—
Though you may have won in all war-storms,
In bloody battles—if you dare wait near
For Grendel in a vigil of nightlong watch."
Beowulf spoke, son of Ecgtheow:
"What, my friend Unferth, drunk with beer,
You have said a bit too much about Breca,
Gabbled on about his feats! I maintain the truth,
That I have had more sea-faring strength,
Suffering on the sea-waves, than any other man:
We two agreed and avowed together
In our boyish boast—we were both then yet
In unripe years—that we two would risk our lives
Out on the sea-waves, and we carried it out so.
When we swam into the sea, we had naked swords,
Hard in our hands: we thought to defend ourselves
Against the whales. Not at all far ahead of me
Could he float faster on the foamy waves,
Nor would I slack off to fall behind him far.
So we two together were on the sea
For five nights, till dashing flood drove us apart,
The surging sea-waves, the coldest of weathers,

12. The Heatho-Ræmas was a people in southern Norway.
13. The Brondings is a tribal name.
14. Breca was son of Beanstan.

Darkening night and the north wind
Battle-grim blew on us; fierce were the waves.
Anger was aroused in the sea creatures.
There my mail-shirt, hard-locked by hand,
Performed protection of me against the predators:
The woven war-wear, embellished with gold,
Lay on my breast. A fiendish foe full of hatred
Fiercely pulled me to the floor of the sea,
Grim in its grip; however, it happened to be granted me
That I attacked the atrocious demon with my dagger,
My battle-sword; the blast of a bloody duel destroyed
The mighty monster of the deep, thanks to my hand.
(IX) So often loathsome creatures perpetrated
Persecution on me pressingly. I paid back to them
With my fine sword, insomuch as fit it was.
They by no means had the pleasure of feasting,
These rapacious ravagers, of ravenously devouring me,
Sitting around a round table, near the seafloor.
But in the morning, wounded by my mace,
They floated up along the foamy shore,
Slaughtered by my sword, that since then never
They prevented the sea-faring men from their passage
Over the soaring sea-waves. Light came from the east,
God's bright beacon; the surging waves subsided,
That I could see the headlands with
The wind-blown walls. Fate often spares a man
Not yet doomed to die, when his daring deserves it!
Anyhow it was my lot that with my sword I slew
Nine nether-water monsters; I have not heard of
A fiercer fight at night beneath the heaven's vault,

Nor of a man put in more miserable state in the sea.
However, I delivered myself from the demons' grip,
Weary of war. Then the sea carried me off,
The flood with its flow onto the land of the Finns,
The surging swells did. No such thing about you
Have I heard say of, so severe sword-slashing,
Such brutal butchering; Breca never yet
In the games of battle, nor either of the two of you,
Has done so daring a deed with shining swords—
Nor do I boast of it much—
Though you became the killer of your own brothers,
Your close kinsmen; for that you will in hell
Endure damnation, though your brain may be bright.
I tell you truly, son of Ecglaf,[15]
That Grendel, that fearful ferocious foe, would never
Have inflicted so many infamous injuries on your lord,
Humiliation on Heorot, had your heart,
Your fervor, been as fierce as you deign to declare.
But he has found out that he need not much fear
Any angry retaliation, repercussion of swishing swords,
From your people, the Scyldings destined for victory.
He takes toll by force, reserving mercy for no man
Of the Danish stock, but he takes delight,
Destroys and dispatches, expects no deterrence
By the Spear-Danes; but I shall show to him
The strength and spirit of the Geats soon now,
How we fight. He who may will walk again
Toward mead in good mood, when the morning light
Of another day, the sun dressed in dazzling rays,
Throws beams from the south over the sons of men!"

15. Ecglaf ("Sword-leaving") was the father of Unferth.

Then glad was the giver of treasure, gray-haired
And brave in battle; the guardian of the Bright-Danes
Could hope for help: the herd of the folk
Had heard from Beowulf a firm and fixed resolution.

There was men's laughter; din made delightful sound,
Words were pleasant. Wealhtheow walked forward,
Queen of Hrothgar, caring of courtesy,
The gold-adorned one greeted the men in the hall,
And the noble lady proffered to pass a cup,
First to the guardian of the land of the East-Danes,
And bade him to be blithe at his beer-drinking,
Beloved of his people. He partook of the pleasure,
The triumphant king did, of the feast and the hall-cup.
Then the woman of the Helmings[16] went round
To each group of men, well-tried warriors and youthful ones,
Offering them the valued vessel, till it came to pass
That she, the gold-adorned queen, the good gracious one,
Brought along the bowl for mead to Beowulf.
She greeted the man of the Geats, thanked God,
Wise in the use of words, since her pleasure had come to pass,
That she might put her trust in one man, who would
Help hinder the heinous butchery. He received that bowl,
The ferocious fighter, from the hand of Wealhtheow,
And then, resolved to fight the fiend, uttered thus—
Beowulf spoke, son of Ecgtheow:
"I made up my mind, when I set out on the sea,
Sat in the sea-boat with the troop of my men,
That I would by all means fulfill the wish
Of your folk, or die in the deadly fight,

16. The Helmings were the clan to which Wealhtheow belonged.

Fast in the fiend's grip. I shall fulfill
A deed worthy of a man; or, let me breathe
My last breath right here in this mead-hall!"
These words well pleased the woman,
Coming from the Geat full of stomach; gold-adorned,
The good queen of folk went to sit beside her sire.
Then were again as before within the hall
Spirited words spoken, people in jollity,
Boisterous sound of boastful folk, till soon afterwards
The son of Healfdene wanted to retire
To bed for the night's rest. He knew of the battle
Appointed by the hateful demon in the high hall,
From the time when they could see the light of the sun
Till night deepening in the dark over all,
The shapes of shadows came, gliding,
Wan under the clouds. The whole host arose.
Then the men greeted one another,
And Hrothgar bade Beowulf the best of luck,
Wielding of the wine-hall, and uttered thus:
"Never before have I yielded to any man,
Since I could lift my hand and a shield,
Rule of the mighty Danish hall, but to you now.
Have now and hold the best of all houses,
Bear in mind the glory, make mighty valor known,
Be wary against the wretch! There will be no want of rewards,
If you succeed in the valorous venture and stay alive."
(X) Then Hrothgar left with his band of retainers,
Prince of the Scyldings did, out of the hall.
The warlord wanted to seek Wealhtheow,
His queen, for his bedfellow: the King of Glory had

Appointed a hall-guardian, as men came to know,
To deal with Grendel; he attended to a special task
Near the lord of the Danes, offered watch against the monster.
Indeed, the man of the Geats had a firm faith
In his spirited strength, and in God's grace.

[671–836: Beowulf keeps vigil in anticipation of his encounter with Grendel; Grendel enters Heorot and devours a warrior; in a handgrip fight Beowulf gives mortal wound to Grendel, who runs away, leaving his arm torn off.]

Then he took off his iron corselet,
The helmet off his head, and handed his adorned sword,
The best of all swords, to his attendant;
And he ordered him to keep guard of the battle-gears.
Then the brave one spoke some boasting words,
Beowulf of the Geats, before he went to bed:
"I do not consider myself poorer in martial prowess
For warlike works, than Grendel himself;
Therefore, I will not put him to sleep with sword,
Deprive him of his life, though quite I may.
He has no recourse that he may better strike me,
Shatter my shield, though he may be strong enough
For his heinous deeds; but we two shall at night
Deal without a sword, if he dares seek
War without weapon; and so may the wise God,
The holy Lord, assign victory on whichever hand,
The way it may seem to be proper to Him."
Then the battle-brave one lay down, a pillow propped
The earl's head, and around him lay down
On the hall floor many a sea-borne brave warrior.

None of them thought that he should from there
Ever seek his dear homeland again—either his folk,
Or fair town where he had been brought up.
But they had heard that cruel death had carried off
Far too many of the Danish people in the mead-hall,
Up till now. But the Lord granted them,
The people of the Weather-Geats, the fortune of
Victory, solace, and support, so that they suppressed
Their foe entirely through one man's strength
And power. The truth has been made known,
That the mighty God has ruled the human race
Always, and ever will.
Striding in the dark night,
The shadowy stroller came. The warriors were sleeping—
Those who should guard the gabled building—
All of them, except one. It was well known to men
That, when the Lord willed it not, the devilish foe
May not draw them beneath the dark shadows.
But watching out for the wretch in wrath,
He waited for the outcome of the fight in fury.
(XI) Then from the moor under the misty slopes came
Grendel, gradually approaching, bearing God's ire.
The direful destroyer of mankind intended
To take one in his grip in that lofty dwelling.
He advanced beneath the clouds to the wine-hall,
Till he most clearly discerned the golden hall
Gleaming with gold plates. Nor was it the first time
For him to seek the home of Hrothgar.
Never in his days of life, neither before nor since,
Had he found the hall-thanes a harder lot to bear.

Then to the hall the marauder made his way,
A stranger to life's joy. The door sprang open,
When his hands gripped the fast-forged bar.
He pulled it open to break the hall-door,
Wrapped up in anger. Then quickly
On the shining floor the fiend stepped,
And walked in, full of anger. In his eyes
Gleamed a flame shooting out an ugly beam.
He saw in the hall many a man of strength,
A band of kinsmen, sleeping together,
A troop of young retainers. Then he exulted
At the thought of tearing, before dawn broke,
Each one's life from his body, as the horrid fiend
Intended, his mouth watering in anticipation
Of a lavish feast. Fate was not so ordained
That he would be allowed to take more of mankind,
When that night was over. The mighty kinsman of Hygelac
Watched out to see how the wicked ravager would
Proceed by attempting a sudden swirl of attack.
The atrocious one did not mean to give any reprieve,
But he promptly took in his grip first
A warrior sound asleep, rent him ravenously,
Bit his bone-locking joints, drank blood pouring out,
Swallowed flesh in sumptuous chunks. He soon had
Gulped down the entire body of the dead man—
Not leaving feet and hands. He stepped forth nearer,
Then seized with his hands the strong-hearted warrior,
Who was reposing. The fiend reached out his hand
Toward Beowulf, who quickly took it in his grip
In undaunted hostility, and sat up, supported by an arm.

Soon the perpetrator of foul deeds perceived
That he had never met, in the middle-earth,
A more powerful handgrip from another man—
Not in this world. He in spirit became afraid,
Felt cowered down in heart; yet he could not get away.
He was intent on freeing himself, wished to flee to his refuge,
And seek the devils' company. What he met there was not
Like what he had found formerly in his days of life.
Then the brave one, Hygelac's kinsman, remembered
His evening speech; he stood upright,
And laid hold on him firmly. Fingers burst;
The giant was striving to escape; the earl stepped further.
The ill-famed one thought, if he could do so,
He would fly to a far-off place and flee away from there
To his fen-retreat: he knew from the grip of the wrathful one
What strength he had. That was a disastrous journey
That the pernicious monster ventured to take to Heorot!

The retainers' hall resounded; to all the Danes,
To the borough-dwellers, to each of the brave ones,
To the earls, terror came. Both of the fierce claimants
Of the hall were in wrath. The building resounded.
Then it was a great wonder that the wine-hall
Withstood the death-defying ones, that the beautiful building
Did not fall to the ground: it was so firmly fastened
Both within and without in iron bands,
With skills allowed to smiths. There from the floor flung,
As I have heard say, many a mead-bench
Adorned with gold, where the enraged grappled.
The wise men of the Danes never before thought of it,
That any of men at any time in any wise could

Break it to bits, splendid and adorned with bone,
Pull asunder with skills, unless an embrace of fire
Would swallow it in flame. A sound rose up,
Utterly unheard of: on the North-Danes swept
Dreadful horror, on each one of them,
Who heard from the wall a mournful wail,
The sound of terrible bellowing of God's enemy,
The cry of defeat, the slave of hell bewailing
The pain he felt. He held the demon firmly,
He who was the strongest in might
Among men in that day of this life.
(XII) The champion of the earls would by no means
Allow the murderous visitor to go away alive,
Nor did he account his own life-days as of use
To any of the people. Then each earl of Beowulf
Quickly drew his time-honored heirloom,
Would defend the life of his lord,
His glorious chief, if he could do so.
The bold-spirited battle-braving men did not know,
They didn't,—when they were engaged in fighting
And intended to hew every part of his body
To seek his soul—, that none of the choicest swords,
Not even the best battle-sword in the world,
Would inflict any harm on that evil-doer,
For by witchcraft he had made the weapons ineffectual,
All of their swords. His departure from life,
No matter what might happen on earth,
Was bound to be miserable; and the accursed spirit
Was to travel far into the realm of the fiends.

Then he who had so far perpetrated many atrocities,

Deeds of affliction of the heart of human race,
Realized that he was in a state of strife against God—
That for him the body would not do much service,
But the high-spirited kinsman of Hygelac
Had him in his grip. Each of them to the other
Was loathsome, being alive. The dire demon had lived
To feel bodily pain. He had received in one shoulder
An undeniable, deadly wound: the sinews sprang asunder,
The bone-locks burst. To Beowulf was given
The glory in battle; mortally wounded, Grendel
Had to flee from there to be under the marshland,
And seek his joyless abode. Therefore, readily he knew
That the end of his life had been reached—
His days were numbered. To all the Danes,
After the bloody fight, jubilee came to pass.
Thus, he who had come from afar earlier,
Wise and strong-spirited, had the hall of Hrothgar
Purged and saved from affliction. For the work at night,
He rejoiced at his heroic deeds. The man of the Geats
Fulfilled the boastful promise he had made to the East-Danes.
Thus, he provided remedy for all the distress
And sorrow, which they had formerly suffered,
And had to endure for the affliction—the tremendous
Torment inflicted on them. That was a clear token,
When the battle-brave one laid the hand down,
Arm and shoulder—there was all together
Grendel's clutching—under the vaulted roof.

[837–990: The Danes rejoice over Grendel's defeat; a thane recounts, on that festive occasion, old tales of Sigemund and of Heremod; Hrothgar gives a

commendatory speech on Beowulf's feat; Beowulf gives an unvarnished report to Hrothgar on how he has overcome Grendel; Unferth remains silent in the presence of the palpable proof of Beowulf's martial prowess.]

(XIII) Then in the morning, as I have heard say,
Many a man gathered there around the gift-hall.
From afar and from near, throughout the wide regions,
The folk-leaders came to watch the wonder,
The traces left by the hateful foe. His parting from life
Did not seem sad to any of the men,
Who beheld the footprints of the defeated—
How he, disheartened, away from there,
Overcome in a battle, into the mere of water-monsters,
Doomed to die and put to flight, bore away his bloody tracks.
There was a pool of water boiling brimful with blood.
Horrid swirl of surfs, all mingled with
Hot pour from gore, was boiling with battle-blood.
Destined for death, he hid in his fen-refuge,
When, deprived of mirth, he gave up his life,
His heathen soul: then hell received him.
　　The old retainers, and many a young one also,
From there made a joyful journey back again,
From the mere, high-spirited, on horseback—
The soldiers on their steeds. There was Beowulf's
Fame extolled; many folks repeatedly said
That, south or north, between the seas,
Over the wide expanse of land, none other
Under the stretch of the sky was a better man
For bearing a shield, or deserved a kingdom more.
Yet they did not find fault with their friendly lord,
Gracious Hrothgar, who was a good king.

Now and again the battle-brave ones let their bay steeds
Gallop and run to compete with one another,
Where the footpaths looked fair, not falling short of
Their fame as fine tracks. At times a thane of the king,
One endowed with eloquence, with a store of stories—
He who remembered a multitude of songs,
A great number of old tales—devised another tale
With well-woven words: he in turn started to
Sing of the feat of Beowulf with eloquence,
And compose a tale successfully with his skills,
With words set anew.

He did not miss anything
In telling what he had heard say of Sigemund's[17]
Deeds of valor, many an unknown tale,
The strife of the son of Wæls, his journeys afar,
The feuds and the evil deeds, of which the offspring of men
Had no knowledge—except Fitela with him,
To whom he would not mind revealing such matters,
As uncle to his nephew: they were companions
Ever so close in every battle they fought together.
They had together defeated many a clan of giants
With their swords. For Sigemund sprang up
Not a little glory after the day of his death,
When, hardy as he was in battle, he killed a serpent
That watched over treasure. Under a gray stone, he,
Son of a prince, ventured all alone upon
The daring deed, nor was Fitela with him.
However, it befell him that the sword pierced
The wondrous worm that it stayed stuck on the wall,

17. Sigemund ("Victory-hand") was the son of Wæls (l. 877), and uncle and father of Fitela (l. 879).

The splendid sword did; the dragon died of the deadly stroke.
The fierce fighter, with his valor, had incurred
That he could rejoice at claiming the ring-hoard,
Upon his own will. He loaded his sea-boat,
Bore into the ship's bosom the dazzling adornments,
Son of Wæls did. The dragon had melted away hot.

He was among heroes the most widely known
Over many nations, a guardian of the warriors,
For his valorous deeds—the cause of his earlier prosperity—
After Heremod's[18] fortune in war became doomed,
When his strength and valor declined: taken by the Jutes,
Heremod was forsworn while in the power of his enemies,
And he was quickly put to death. Swelling sorrows had
Oppressed him too long; he had been to his people,
To all princes, source of lifelong care;
Also many a wise man often lamented, in earlier times,
The venture the strong-spirited man had undertaken—
Those who counted on him as remedy for the tribulations,
And hoped that the prince's son would prosper,
Receive the legacy from his father, guard the people,
Treasure, and the stronghold, the kingdom of warriors,
The land of the Scyldings.—He,[19] the kinsman of
Hygelac, there became dearer to his friends,
To all of human race; sin had gotten hold of Heremod.

At times, competing on horseback, they raced
On the sandy roads, when the morning light
Had approached and hastened. Many a retainer,
Firmly resolved, went to the high hall

18. Heremod ("Army-courage") was a king of the Danes.
19. "He" refers to Beowulf.

To see the strange wonder; the king himself,
The guardian of the treasure-hoards with fame for virtues,
Also carried his steps in triumph from his conjugal quarter,
Attended by a large retinue; and his queen with him,
Followed by a train of waiting ladies, trod the path to the mead-hall.
(XIV) Hrothgar spoke—he had gone to the hall,
Stood on the steps, watched the steep roof
Glittering with gold, and also Grendel's hand—:
    "For this sight, let thanks be given at once
To the Ruler! I have suffered much from the loathsome foe,
Great torment from Grendel: God may always work
Wonder after wonder, the Guardian of glory may.
It was not long ago that I did not expect
Ever to live to see remedy for any of the miseries
For me, when the best of dwellings stood
Besmeared with blood, dreary with dripping gore—
Woe widespread for every one of my wise men,
Those who did not expect that they could ever
Defend the folk's fortress from the fiendish foes,
Demons and vile spirits. Now a warrior has,
Through the Lord's might, performed a deed
That we all could not accomplish before
With our abilities. Indeed, whoever the woman
Who gave birth to that son of hers, amongst all men,
May say, if she be still alive, that the God of old
Granted special grace on her, when she was
About to bear a child. Now, Beowulf,
Best of men, I will love you in my heart,
As a father does his son. From now on, keep well
This new kinship. You will not lack anything,

Of all the worldly goods I have in my possession.
Very often I have bestowed reward for less,
Have honored with gifts a man of less worth,
Less bold in battle. With your own deeds you have
Made it clear that your glory will for evermore
Live on. May the Almighty reward you
With goodness, as He even now has done!"
    Beowulf spoke, son of Ectheow:
"We have more than willingly done the daring work,
The fight, and have boldly braved whatever force
The unknown foe might have. I would rather wish
That you could have seen his very presence,
The fiend in all his flourishes, fallen so low!
I thought that I would bind him quickly
On his death-bed with my deadly grip,
That he, on account of my hand-grip, would soon
Be writhing, panting for life, unless his body had escaped.
I could not, since God did not will it so,
Keep him from going, nor did I hold him hard enough,
The deadly foe: the fiend was too full of force
To be kept in my grip. However, he let his hand
Stay behind as his trace, to preserve his life,
Arm and shoulder; neither thereby, even so,
The cursed creature secured any comfort;
Nor will the loathsome ravager live the longer,
Afflicted by his crimes; but pain has seized
Him tightly in its inexorable grip,
With relentless locks; the creature there bearing
The marks of crime must await the grand doom,
What the Lord of light will decree for him."

Then the son of Ecglaf[20] became more reticent a man,
In boastful outpour on battle-brave deeds,
After the nobles had beheld the hand
Put high over the roof by the strength of an earl,
The fingers of the fiend; to look at from the front,
Each of the strong nails was most like steel;
The horrible hand-spur of the heathen harasser
Was frightening; everyone said that no sword,
No matter how hard and well brandished,
Would harm him, that it would have made
The bloody atrocities subside, of the brutish fiend.

[991–1250: The Danes restore Heorot destroyed by Grendel's rampage; Hrothgar bestows bounteous gifts on Beowulf and his band; a minstrel recites the tale of a feud between the Scyldings and the Frisians; Wealhtheow makes a wish for good future term between her sons and her nephew, and presents jewels to Beowulf; the feast ends, and everyone retires for the night.]

(XV) Then it was ordered that Heorot be inwardly
Bedecked quickly by hands; there was quite a number
Of men and women who made ready the wine-hall,
The banquet-building. Gold-adorned tapestries shone
On the walls, many a wondrous scene
To each man, who gazes on such a sight!
That bright building had been utterly broken—
The whole interior fastened firm by steel bands—
With its hinges cracked. The roof alone remained
Undamaged entirely, which the demonic fiend,
Guilty of gruesome gore, had left in his flight,

20. "the son of Ecglaf" is Unferth.

Despairing of life. That is not easy
To flee from—let him try who wishes so—,
But he shall seek by necessity
The prepared place, destined for the soul-bearers,
The children of men, the inhabitants of the earth,
Where his body, after the feast of life, will sleep
Fast in the bed of death.
Then time was ripe
That Healfdene's son[21] should walk to the hall;
The king himself would partake of the banquet.
I have not heard of people in a greater band,
Who behaved better in attending to their ring-giver.
Then on the bench sat down the glorious ones.
They rejoiced at the feast; their kinsmen,
The high-spirited Hrothgar and Hrothulf,[22]
Pleasantly partook of many a mead-cup,
In the lofty pavilion. Heorot was within
Filled with friends: in those days the Danes were
Not prone to practice perfidy at all.
Then the son of Healfdene gave to Beowulf
A golden flag of victory as a gift,
An adorned battle-banner, a helmet and a coat of mail;
Many people saw the glorious treasure-sword
Be borne to the hero. Beowulf received
A cup in the hall; for the dispensing of the costly gifts
He had no cause to be baffled in the presence of the warriors.
I have not heard of any other multitude of men
In any other ale-bench who have made a present

21. "Healfdene's son" is Hrothgar.

22. Hrothulf is the son of Halga, Hrothgar's younger brother.

Of the four treasures in a manner more friendly.
Around the top of the helmet the rim held
A head-protection outside, bound with metal bands,
That a storm-sweeping sword could not inflict
A severe injury on its wearer, when the warrior
Should make onward move towards his hostile foes.
Then the guardian of the earls ordered to lead
Into the hall eight horses with gold-plated headgears,
Inside the precincts; on one of them stood
A saddle skillfully decorated and adorned with jewels.
That was the war-seat of the high king,
When the son of Healfdene would perform
The play of swords; never in the front failed
The valor of the valiant, each time the vanquished fell.
And then to Beowulf the prince of Ing's kinsmen[23]
Granted the power to wield on both, the horses
And the weapons; he ordered him to use them well.
So manfully did the glorious prince,
The hoard-guard of men, recompense for the battle-storms
With horses and treasures, that nobody will ever disparage them—
None who wishes to tell the truth after what is correct.
(XVI) Furthermore, on each of the warriors
Who had undertaken the journey with Beowulf,
The prince at the mead-bench bestowed treasure,
An heirloom; and he ordered to recompense him
With gold—the one whom Grendel had earlier
Slaughtered savagely—as he[24] would have done more,
Had God in His wisdom and the hero's high spirit

23. Ing was a legendary king of Denmark; hence "Ing's kinsmen"—"Ingwina" (l. 1043)—means "the Danes."

24. "he" refers to Grendel.

Not forestalled that fate. The Lord has ruled over
The whole of mankind, as He even now does.
Therefore, prudence, forethought of mind,
At all times is best. Many of the beloved and the loathed
He shall live to see—he who for long here
In these days of hardship still enjoys the world!
    There was song and music all mixed together
In the presence of Healfdene's battle-leader;[25]
Harp strings strummed, song often sung,
When Hrothgar's minstrel had to recite in the hall,
Along the mead-benches, his entertaining lines:

". . . the retainers of Finn. When a sudden assault swept on them,
The hero of the Half-Danes, Hnæf of the Scyldings,
Was fated to fall on the Frisian field of slaughter.[26]
Not indeed had Hildeburh any reason to praise
The faithfulness of Finn's people; faultless, she became
Deprived of her dear ones at the dashing of shields,
A son and a brother: they fell into fate,
Slaughtered by spears—that was a sorrowful woman.
Not without cause did the daughter of Hoc[27]
Deplore the decree of destiny, when morning came.
Then she could see under the sky the butchery
Of her blood-kin, where she[28] used to bathe in the best bliss
The world had bestowed. The battle had carried off
All the thanes of Finn, leaving only a few,

25. "Healfdene's battle-leader" refers to Hrothgar.

26. As the narrator's sympathy is with the Danish side, the Jutes are being blamed for the outbreak of the fray.

27. Hnæf, king of the Danes, visited his sister Hildeburh, who was queen of Finn the Jute. Hoc, former king of the Danes, was father of Hnæf and Hildeburh.

28. That is Hildeburh.

That he could not in the sword-crossing stead
Carry on combat at all against Hengest,[29]
Nor save the survivors in the war
From the prince's thane; but they tendered the terms:[30]
That they would yield to them another building entirely,
The hall and its high seat, so that they might own
Control of its half with the sons of the Jutes,
And at treasure-dispensing Folcwalda's son[31]
Should honor the Danes on every occasion,
And treat the troop of Hengest with rings—
With just so much quantity of treasure
Of ornamented gold that he would cheer up
The Frisian folk while within the banquet hall.
"Then they confirmed the fast compact of peace
On both sides: Finn declared to Hengest
In oaths with an undisputed zeal,
That he would keep the survivors honorably,
After his councilors' decree, that any man there
Would not break the pact in words or deeds,
Nor would ever complain through evil intent, though
They, bereft of their prince, should follow the slayer
Of their ring-giver, when they were compelled by need;
In case any of the Frisians were to recollect
The murderous hate in speech smacking of audacity,
Then it should be settled by the edge of a sword.
"The funeral pyre was made ready, and gold

29. Hengest led Hnæf's army after the latter's death.

30. It is not clear which side first proffered truce; but in view of the predicament Finn was in, after losing most of his thanes, we can surmise that the Jutes were the ones who wanted a peace treaty. The phrase "the prince's thane" refers to Hengest.

31. "Folcwalda's son" refers to Finn.

Brought from the hoard; the best of the warriors
Of the Scyldings[32] was ready on the funeral pyre.
At the funeral pile clearly discernible was
The bloodstained mail-shirt, all-golden image of boar,
The iron-hard boar-figure on helmet; many a prince
Was destroyed by wounds; many a one died in the slaughter.
Then Hildeburh ordered at Hnæf's funeral fire
To commit her own son to the flame,
To burn the bodies, and place him in the fire
Near his uncle shoulder to shoulder: the woman mourned,
And lamented with plaintive songs; the warrior ascended.[33]
The greatest of funeral fires wound to the skies,
Roared before the barrow; heads melted,
Gashes burst open, while blood poured out,
Grievous wounds of body. The flame swallowed up all—
Most ravenous of spirits—of those that war had carried off
From both peoples: their life force was gone.
(XVII) "Then the warriors, bereft of friends, departed
To go to their dwelling-place—homestead and stronghold—
And seek Friesland. Hengest still stayed on
With Finn for the slaughter-stained winter,
Though unwilling he was. He thought of his land,
Though he could not set sail on the sea
His ring-prowed ship—the sea surged with storm,
Contended with wind; winter locked up the waves
With icy bond, till another year came

32. "The best of the warriors of the Scyldings" refers to Hnæf.

33. "The warrior" should refer to Hildeburh's son, rather than Hnæf. The word "ascended" ("āstāg" in OE) carries with it the connotation of ascending a throne. Although the word may simply mean being lifted up to be put on the pyre, Hildeburh's mourning cannot be only for bereavement: she also laments the death of one who could have become a king in time.

Unto their dwellings—so does it even now,
Glorious bright weather marks the season,
Punctually as ever. Then the winter was gone,
Fair the lap of earth, the exile was eager to depart,
The visitor from the dwelling; he thought more
About revenge for injury than about sea-journey,
If he could bring about a hostile encounter,
So that he might deal with the Jutes' sons by his sword.
Thus he did not refuse the way of the world,[34]
When the son of Hunlaf[35] put on his lap
A battle-beam, the best of swords;
Its blades were well known among the Jutes.
Thus a cruel death by sword befell again
The bold-spirited Finn at his own home,
When Guthlaf and Oslaf[36] related the grim attack,
The grief after the sea-journey, and charged
For their great share of woes; restless mind might not
Be constrained in heart. Then the hall became crimson
With the blood of enemies; also Finn was slain,
King of the band, and the queen was taken.
The Danish warriors carried to the ships
All the household stuffs of the king of the land
And all the precious jewels they could find
At Finn's dwelling. They brought the noble lady

34. "The way of the world" can mean "the common practice," that is, revenging a kinsman's death.

35. From the context one can surmise that Hunlaf was a Danish thane killed in the fight against the Jutes. Hunlaf's son, as a ceremonial gesture, placed his father's sword on Hengest's lap, either to pledge loyalty to him, or to demand him to avenge his father's death. The word "his" refers to Hengest.

36. Guthlaf and Oslaf were probably thanes who had accompanied Hnæf in his voyage to Finnsburh.

To the Danes on a voyage, and
Led her to their people."

The lay was sung,
Tale told by a gleeman. Mirth was renewed again,
The convivial noise sounded loud, the cupbearers poured
Wine from the wonder-bowls. Then forth came Wealhtheow,
Wearing a golden diadem, to where the brave twain
Sat, nephew and uncle;[37] then their friendship was still fair,
Each true to the other. There also Unferth the court-speaker
Sat at the feet of the Danish lord; each of them trusted his spirit,
That he had much courage, though he had been unkind to his kinsmen
At times of sword-blow.[38] Then the queen of the Scyldings spoke:
"Receive this cup, my noble lord,
Dispenser of treasure! Be you now in mirth,
Prince of men; and speak to the Geatish people
With kind words, as a man must do!
Be gracious to the Geats, mindful of their gifts
You now have near and far.
A man told me that you would have a warrior
For your son. Heorot has been purged,
The bright ring-hall; enjoy many rewards
While you can, and leave people and kingdom

37. "nephew and uncle" allude to Hrothulf and Hrothgar, respectively. The ensuing words—"then their friendship was still fair, Each true to the other"—make the reader recall a previous passage: "Heorot was within Filled with friends: in those days the Danes were Not prone to practice perfidy at all" (ll. 1017b–19). The implication is that Hrothulf, son of Hrothgar's younger brother Halga, later acted with disloyalty toward his uncle and liege-lord Hrothgar.

38. What is said here reminds the reader of Beowulf's former accusation of Unferth as a killer of close kinsmen: "Though you became the killer of your own brothers, Your close kinsmen; for that you will in hell endure damnation, though your brain may be bright" (ll. 587–89).

To your kinsmen, when you must go forth
And see the decree of fate. I know my kind Hrothulf,
Son of Halga, will keep the young men
For the sake of honor, if you before he,
Lord of the Scyldings, leave the world.
I expect that he will repay our offspring
With goodness, if he remembers all that—
What favors we earlier did for him as a child,
For the sake of pleasure and honor."[39]
Then she went to the bench where her sons were,
Hrethric and Hrothmund, and the warriors' sons,
The youths together; there the brave man sat—
Beowulf of the Geats—close by the two brothers.
(XVIII) To him a cup was borne, and friendship
Offered in words, and twisted gold bestowed
With good wishes, along with two arm-ornaments,
Corselet, and rings, the greatest of neck-rings
That I have ever heard about on earth.
I have not heard of any better jewel of men
Under the sky, since Hama carried
To the bright burg a necklace of the Brosings,
A broach and a cup—fled the treacherous enmity
Of Eormenric, and chose an eternal benefit.[40]

39. That is, "For the sake of [our] pleasure and [his] honor."

40 Both Hama and Eormenric are names mentioned a few times in *Widsith*, and the latter appears again in *Deor*. But the contexts in which they appear in these shorter poems are too obscure to throw light on what these few lines are about. Probably the Anglo-Saxon audience was familiar with the tale of Hama and Eormenric, about whom a matching tale may be found in a Northern saga:

> Heimir [Hama] was a retainer of Thithrekr [Theodoric], nephew to Erminrekr [Eormenric], to whom also he had alleged loyalty. When Erminrekr banished Thithrekr, Heimir rebelled against the former, and led the life of an outlaw, intent on harassing him by stealing his treasures

This ring Hygelac of the Geats, nephew[41] to Swerting,
Had—he had it till most recently—
When under a banner he defended the treasure,
And protected the battle-spoil. Fate took him away,
When he, out of pride, sought for trouble—
Feud with the Frisians. He carried the treasures,
The mighty prince did carry the precious stones
Over the sea brimful of waves; he fell under a shield.
Then the king's body passed into the Franks' possession,[42]
And his breast-guard and the ring, along with it;
The lowly warmongers plundered those slain,
When carnage was over; the people of the Geats kept
The place filled with bodies.
The hall overflowed with sound.
Wealhtheow spoke, she spoke before the company:
"Enjoy this ring, Beowulf, my dear young man,
With prosperity, and enjoy wearing this corselet,
These treasures of people, and prosper well.
Prove yourself with power, and be kind to these boys
In your counsel! I will think of a reward for you for that.
You have brought it about, that far and near

> and killing his followers. Having spent two full decades as a drifter, Heimir, aggrieved of his wasted life, entered a monastery, bequeathing all he had to the sanctuary for his future refuge. (Cf. George Jack, *Beowulf: A Student Edition*, 100, note.)

The "necklace of the Brosings" is known to have been worn by the goddess Freya (or Freyja), and been stolen by Loki, according to a Northern saga. The *Beowulf*-poet makes Hama the one who took the necklace from Eormenric's hoard. (Cf. Jack, *Beowulf: A Student Edition*, 101, note.) The phrase "an eternal benefit" (l. 1201) may allude to Hama's retreat into a sanctuary for his soul's rest.

41. The word "nefa" (l. 1203 in MS) can mean either "nephew" or a "grandson."

42. Later in the poem (ll. 2172–76) Beowulf presents the necklace to Hygd, Hygelac's queen, after his return to his homeland. Here it is said that Hygelac was wearing it during his assault on the Frisians; and upon his death it fell into the possession of the Franks.

People will praise you forever and ever,
Even so widely as does the sea, home of the winds,
Surround the walls. While you live, prince,
Be prosperous! I wish you to keep the treasures,
Being duly yours. Be you to my son
Kind in deeds, being so blessed!
Here is each earl faithful to the other,
Kind in heart, loyal to his liege lord.
The thanes are united, people all-willing;
Flushed with wine, the retainers do as I bid."

Then she returned to her seat. A banquet best in its kind
Went on, in which men drank heartily. They were not aware
Of the grim fate, as it happened to befall
Many of the earls when the evening came;
And the mighty Hrothgar left for his dwelling
To rest for the night; innumerable earls guarded
The hall, as they often had done before.
They cleared the benches away; it became overspread
With beds and cushions. One of the drunken feasters
Lay down on a hall-couch, ready to receive death as his doom.
They had set battle-shields, bright wooden boards,
As pillows. There on the bench were
Over the prince clearly visible
A helmet towering battle-worthy, a corselet woven of rings,
And a spear most warlike. It was their practice
That they were always prepared for battle,
Both at home and in the field, and at any of such
Times as when a trouble had befallen their liege,
Distress coming unexpected; the troop was a good one.

[1251–1496: Grendel's mother makes an assault on Heorot, and kills Æschere; Hrothgar requests Beowulf to rid of him of the female monster; they go to the mere of Grendel and his mother; Beowulf puts on armor, and bids farewell to Hrothgar before plunging into the mere.]

(XIX) Then they fell asleep. One paid heavily for
His evening rest, as it had happened to them so often
When Grendel ransacked the golden hall,
Perpetrated misdeed till the end came—
Death after his devilish deeds. It became obvious and
Widely known to men that an avenger still
Lived after the loathsome one for a long time,
After the bloody duel: Grendel's mother—
A fiendish female monster—bore in mind the misery,
She who had to inhabit the dreadful water,
The cold streams, when Cain came to be
The sword-slayer of his sole brother—a branch of
The same fatherly root; he then roamed away outlawed,
Fleeing from life's joy among men, marked for murder,
And inhabited a wasteland. From him sprang many
Of the fate-engendered spirits: Grendel was one of them,
The hateful accursed foe that found at Heorot
The watchful warrior awaiting warlike confrontation;
There the fiend laid hold of the one waiting for him.
However, the latter remembered the strength of power,
The bountiful gift, which God had granted him,
And entrusted himself to the Lord for His help,
Solace and support; thus, he overcame the fiend,
And had the hell's demon subdued. Then he left humiliated,
Deprived of mirth, to see the place of his death—

The enemy of mankind did. And yet his mother,
Greedy and gloomy, wanted to embark upon
A venture perilous and avenge her son's death.

Then she came to Heorot, where the Ring-Danes
Were sleeping all over the hall; then there soon occurred
Turmoil for the earls, when Grendel's mother
Dashed into the hall. The horror was the less,
Even to such a degree as should female strength be,
The warlike threat of a woman, than a warrior's,
When a ring-adorned hammer-forged sword,
A blood-besmeared bill with strong blades,
Cuts the boar over the helmet an opponent wears.[43]
Then in the hall hard-edged sword was drawn
Over the seats; many a broad shield firm
Was heaved by hand; none could remember his helmet
Or his broad corselet, once terror had gotten hold of him.
She was in haste, and wanted to go out from there,
To save her life, when she was discovered.
Quickly she had one of the men seized
Firmly; then she went to her marshland.
He was the man dearest to Hrothgar
In the position of a retainer on earth,
A valiant shield-bearer, a glorious warrior,
That she killed while in rest. Beowulf was not there,
For a separate lodge had earlier been prepared
For the glorious Geat, when the ring-giving was done.
Outcry arose in Heorot; she had taken, besmeared in blood,

43. As the poem progresses, we realize that Grendel's mother was a much more fearsome opponent for Beowulf than Grendel. By saying that those sleeping at Heorot, though terrorized by the sudden assault of Grendel's mother, underestimated her ferocity as a formidable assailant on account of her sex, the poet makes the horror they had to face later even greater. A touch of twisted understatement!

The well-known hand;[44] care was renewed,
Coming upon the dwelling. That was not a fair deal,
That they, on both sides, had to pay
With the lives of friends!
Then the old king,
The hoary warrior, was in a troubled mind,
Since he knew that his chief thane
Was no longer alive, his dearest one dead.
Speedily to the hall Beowulf was sent for,
The victorious man was. As soon as the day broke,
The noble champion, one of the heroes, went
With his retainers to where the wise man was waiting
To see whether the Lord would ever for him
Bring forth a remedy after the woeful tidings.
Then the battle-brave man walked in on the hall floor,
With his troop—the hall-wood resounded—
So that he might address the wise lord
Of the friends of Ing[45] in words, ask if to him
The night had been agreeable after his desires.
(XX) Hrothgar spoke, protector of the Scyldings:
"Do not ask about joys! Sorrow is renewed
To the Danish people: Æschere is dead,
Yrmenlaf's elder brother,
My trusted confidant and my counselor,
My comrade—when we in battle protected our
Respective heads, and when the foot-troops clashed,
Dashed against the helmet boars; so should a warrior be,
A man good from old times, as Æschere was!

44. "The well-known hand" is that of Grendel.
45. "the friends of Ing" are the Danes.

A wandering murderous sprite has slain him
With her hands in Heorot: I do not know to where
The horrid one took her trip back, glorying in her carrion,
Rejoicing at the feast. She has done revenge on the fight,
In which yesterday night you killed Grendel
In a violent manner with your strong grips,
Because he had dwindled and destroyed my people
Much too long; in the fight he fell down,
Having his life forfeited. And now another
Powerful evil-doer came, would avenge her son,
And has so far made vengeance for the fight—
As it may appear to many a thane,
Who weeps in his heart for his treasure-giver,
A hard heart-bale; now the hand lies low,
That treated you well with all the good things.[46]
“I have heard the land-dwellers, my people,
The hall-counselors say so—
That they have seen such two huge
Wanderers in the wasteland, the accursed spirits,
Hold the marshes. One of them was,

46 The MS reads: “nū sēo hand ligeð/ sē þe ēow wēlhwylcra wilna dohte” (“now the hand lies [low]/ That treated you well with all the good things”).

Scholars have taken “the hand” as that of Æschere—under the supposition that Hrothgar laments that, now that Æschere is dead, the latter can no longer provide the help he used to while alive. Thus, Donaldson’s prose translation reads: “Now the hand lies lifeless that was strong in support of all your desires.” And George Jack, in his note, remarks: “Although the antecedent of sē þe ‘which’ is the feminine noun hand (1343), the reference is to Æschere; this is probably why the masculine pronoun sē has been used” (Jack, *Beowulf: A Student Edition*, 108, note).

I strongly object to the above reading. The preceding lines read: “As it may appear to many a thane,/ Who weeps in his heart for his treasure-giver,/ A hard heart-bale;” (“þæs þe þincean mæg þegne monegum,/ sē þe æfter sincgyfan on sefan grēoteþ,— / hreþerbealo hearde;”) (ll. 1341–43a). The point is that Hrothgar’s thanes feel at a loss in the presence of his inability to find a solution. “The hand [that] lies low,” which used to treat the thanes well, is not Æschere’s but *Hrothgar’s;* Hrothgar is lamenting his being helpless in spite of his favorite thane Æschere’s death.

According to what they most certainly could know,
In the likeness of a woman; the other wretch
Trod his tracks of exile in the shape of a man,
Except that he was bigger than any other man.
The earth-dwellers called him Grendel
In olden days. They don't know who fathered him,
Whether any before him had been begotten
Of dark spirits. They inhabit a hidden land—
Wolf-infested slopes, windy headlands, and
A perilous fen-path, where the mountain-stream
Falls down in the mist from the headlands
And flows beneath the earth. Not far from here,
A few miles away, stands the mere,
Over which droop trees covered with frost.
The wood darkens the water with entangled roots.
There every night a fearful wonder is seen—
Fire flaring on the water. None alive among men,
No matter how wise, knows how deep it is.
Fleeing from far off, chased by hounds, a stag
May seek a holt-wood to hide his strong horns;
Yet he will rather give up his life, lingering
On the bank, than plunge his head into the pool
To save his life;[47] that is not a pleasant place!
From there surging waves rise up,
Darkening the clouds, while the wind swirls,
Threatening storms, till the air turns choking
And the sky howls. Now the remedy is at hand

47. The MS reads: "ær he in wille hafelan:" (Zupitza's transliteration). Klaeber read the two hemistichs: "ær hē in wille, hafelan [beorgan];" Dobbie emended them: "ær he in wille hafelan hydan." There is not much difference in meaning between "preserving one's head" (Klaeber) and "hiding one's head" (Dobbie). So we might provide the eclectic translation: "than plunge his head into the pool to save his life," as I have done.

Again only from you. You don't know the dwelling yet,
The dangerous place, where you might find
The sinful creature; seek if you dare!
I will reward you with riches for the fight,
With ancient treasures, as I have done before,
With twisted gold, if you come away."
(XXI) Beowulf spoke, son of Ecgtheow:
"Do not be in grief, wise man! It is better for any man
That he avenge his friend than he mourn much.
Each of us must live to see the end
Of worldly life; let him, who may, attain glory
Before his death: that is best for a fighting man,
After he has done with his living days to leave behind.
Arise, guardian of the kingdom. Let us go quickly
And see the track of Grendel's kinswoman.
I promise you this: she will not escape into a refuge,
Nor into the bosom of the earth, nor into a mountain-wood,
Nor to the bottom of the sea, go where she may!
This day do have patience
For each of the woes, as I hope you will."
    Then the old man leapt up, thanked God,
The mighty Lord, for what the man had spoken.
For Hrothgar then a horse was saddled—
The steed with braided mane. The wise king
Rode in a stately manner; a troop on foot marched,
The band of shield-bearers. The footprints were
Clearly traceable along the woodland paths,
The track over the ground, where she had gone straight
Over the dark moor, bearing the best
Of thanes no longer blessed with soul—

Of those who had with Hrothgar kept watch over home.
Then the offspring of noble princes[48] traversed
Steep stony slopes, narrow lanes,
Deserted paths, an unknown trail,
Precipitous headlands, many an abode of water-monsters;
He rode ahead with a handful of his
Wise counselors to investigate the terrain,
Till he suddenly found the mountain trees
Leaning over a gray stone—
A wood deprived of joy. Water stagnated underneath—
Dreary and turbid; to all the Danes,
The retainers of the Scyldings, to many thanes,
It was painful in heart to endure, to each of the men
It was a moment of grief, when they saw
Æschere's head put on the cliff by the waterside.
The water was bubbling with blood—people saw—
Hot still. The horn sounded time and again
The war song prepared. The entire troop sat down.
    Then they saw in the water many of the serpents' kin
And sinister sea-snakes swimming in the pool,
Also the water-monsters lying on the headlands,
Which in the morning-tide often venture on a
Perilous journey in the sea: those serpents and wild beasts.
They rushed on the way, fierce and enraged:
They had heard the sound, the war-horn singing.
A man of the Geats deprived one of them
Of life with an arrow shot from his bow,
Of its sinew for swimming, for the strong war-arrow .
Stuck in it for life; it was in the water

48 "the offspring of noble princes" refers to Hrothgar.

Slower in swimming, for it was now in the grip of death.
Speedily it was ransacked hard on the waves
With sword-hooked barbed boar-spears,
Assailed violently, and drawn to the bluff—
The wonder-causing wave-roamer; people beheld
The horrid monster. Beowulf put on
His armor; he had no anxiety about his life;
The battle-corselet woven link by link by hand,
Broad and bearing crafty design, should now delve into water—
The armor that could protect his body
So that no hostile grasp might harm his breast,
Nor any malicious grip of an angry one might injure his life;
But the glittering helmet protected the head—
The helmet that should scour the floors of the mere
And visit the vortex—being adorned with treasure
And encircled with splendid bands, as the weapon-smith
Wrought it in olden days, shaping it wondrously,
Adorning it with boar-figures, so that since then
No sword or battle-maces could batter it.
Then it was not the smallest of mighty helps
That Hrothgar's court speaker[49] lent him in need:
The hilted sword was called Hrunting.
That was an old legacy of ancient treasury.
Its blade was iron, decorated with poison-stripes,
And hardened with bloodshed; never at battle it had
Failed any of those who wielded it in their hands—
One that dared to enter upon perilous expeditions,
And run into a crowd of swarming foes. It was not
The first time that it should enact a work of valor.

49. "Hrothgar's court speaker" is Unferth.

Indeed, the son of Ecglaf,[50] of mighty strength,
Did not remember what he had earlier spoken,
Drunk with wine, when he lent the weapon
To a better warrior. He himself dared not
Risk his life under the turbulence of waves
To perform bravery; there he lost his glory,
Fame for courage. It was not so with the other,
When he had made himself all ready for the fight.
(XXII) Beowulf spoke, son of Ecgtheow:
"Think now, glorious son of Healfdene,
Wise king, now that I am ready for the venture,
Prince of men, of what we two talked about earlier:
That, if at your need I should lose my life,
You would always be in the place of a father
For me, when I am gone.
Be you the guardian of my young retainers,
My companions, if the battle should carry me off.
Also, the treasures that you have given me,
Dear Hrothgar, send them to Hygelac.
Then the lord of the Geats will perceive on the gold,
The son of Hrethel will, when he looks on that treasure,
That I had found a good ring-giver
With manly virtues, and enjoyed while I could.
And let Unferth the wide-known man have
The old heirloom, the splendid sword with ornaments,
Hard of edge; I will attain glory
With Hrunting, or death will carry me off!"
After these words the man of the Weather-Geats
Hastened with courage—he would not wait

50. "the son of Ecglaf" is Unferth.

For an answer: the surge of the water received
The warrior. Then was it a long while of the day
That he could see the floor of the mere.

[1497–1590: Beowulf scuffles with a female water-monster, and arrives at the underwater pavilion of Grendel and his mother; he fights Grendel's mother, and finally beheads her with the giants-made sword he finds in the hall; Beowulf decapitates Grendel to complete his victory.]

Soon that which had occupied the watery region
For half of a hundred years, fiercely ravenous,
Grim and greedy, found that there a certain man
From above was exploring the dwelling of the demons.
She then gripped and seized the warrior towards her
With her horrid clutches; yet she could not injure
The wholesome body inside; the ring-mail protected outside,
That she could not pierce the battle-wear,
The shirt of interlocked rings, with her loathsome fingers.
Then the she-wolf of the sea, when she came to the bottom,
Brought the prince of the rings to her dwelling.
So he could not—no matter how brave he was—
Wield his weapons; but many of the monsters molested him
In the water, and many of the underwater brutes
Battered his battle-wear with their bulging tusks,
The fiends followed him. Then the warrior perceived
That he was in a certain hall of hostility,
Where no downpour of water would fall on him,
Nor a sudden sweep of flood could drown him,
For the hall was roofed. He saw fire-light,
A blazing gleam burn brightly.

Then the brave man saw the accursed of the deep,
The mighty mere-woman; he gave such powerful swing
To his battle-sword—his hand did not deny the blow—
That the ring-sword, falling on her head, made
A grim sound. Then the visitor found out
That the sword would not serve its purpose,
Injure life, but the sword had failed to serve
The prince in his need; many a hand-grapple it had
Gone through earlier, and often cut through the helmet
And fight-wear of the fated; it was the first time
For the fine treasure when its glory had failed.
Still he was determined; Hygelac's kinsman was
Not loose in courage, but intent on attaining glory.
He threw away the sword bound with carved ornaments—
The angry warrior did—that it lay on the ground,
Strong and steel-edged; he counted on his own strength,
The handgrip of his might. So must a man act,
When in a battle he thinks of obtaining the glory
That will last long; he did not care about his life.

Then the man of the War-Geats gripped Grendel's
Mother by her shoulder; he never shrank from the fight.
Then the battle-brave one, when he was enraged,
Did fling the deadly fiend, and she fell on the floor.
She speedily paid back for his painful punishment
With her grim grips, and grappled with him.
Then the strongest of fighters, the foot-warrior,
Stumbled in exhaustion, and he happened to fall.
Then she sat upon the hall-visitor, and drew her short sword,
Broad and bright-edged; she wanted to avenge her son,
Her sole offspring. On his shoulder lay

The woven mail-shirt, which protected his life;
It prevented sharp point and edge from piercing.
Thus the son of Ecgtheow, the champion of the Geats,
Might have perished under the wide plain of earth,
Had his battle-wear not lent him help—
The hard metal-woven net—and the Holy God
Brought about victory; the Lord in His wisdom,
The Ruler of the heavens, rightly decided it
With ease, for he stood up again.
(XXIII) Then he saw among the battle-gear a ferocious falchion,
An ancient sword with strong edges, made by giants—
The glory of warriors. That was the best of weapons,
Except that it was greater than any other man
Could bear to battle for warlike wielding,
Strong and splendid, wrought by giants.
He gripped the linked hilt—the hero of the Scyldings did—
Rough and fierce; he drew the ring-sword,
Despairing of life, angrily struck,
That it dug into her deep on the neck,
And broke the bone-ring; the falchion went smartly through
The body of the fated; she fell on the floor.
The bill was bloody, the man rejoiced at his work.
The gleam brightened, while the light stayed within,
Even as the candle of the sky shines clearly
From the heaven. He looked around the hall;
Then he walked along the wall, and lifted the weapon
Hard by the hilt—the thane of Hygelac,
In anger and determination. The sword was not useless
To the warrior; but he wished to pay back
Speedily to Grendel for many of the assaults

Which he had perpetrated on the West-Danes,
Much too often—more than on one occasion,
When he slew Hrothgar's hearth-companions
While asleep, and devoured the sleeping
Fifteen men of the Danish folk,
And carried off another such number,
As hideous booties. For that he paid him requital—
The wrathful warrior did—when he saw Grendel
Lying lifeless, as if in rest, wornout with war—
So much had he been injured beforehand
From the fight at Heorot. The body spread wide,
When he suffered a blow after death,
The strong sweep of the sword, and his head fell, chopped off.

[1591-1798: Those waiting at the waterside despair, upon seeing the blood bubbling up; the fiends' blood melts down the sword-blade, and Beowulf swims back to the shore with his booties, Grendel's head and the hilt of the sword; Beowulf returns to Heorot with his band to present his booties to Hrothgar; Beowulf greets Hrothgar, ascribing his victory to God's grace; Hrothgar gives a commendatory speech to Beowulf, warning him of misrule and disregard of divine providence; they feast and retire to bed for the night.]

Soon the wise men saw—
Those who with Hrothgar were gazing on the water—
That the tossing wave was entirely stirred up,
Bubbling with blood. The gray-haired ones,
The aged men around the good king, spoke in unison
That they could not hope to see the prince again—
Expect that he would come back victorious to seek
The glorious king: then many men decided that

Surely the she-wolf of the mere had killed him.
Then the ninth hour of the day came. The valiant Danes
Left the headland; the prince of the men departed
For home from there. The visitors sat,
Downcast in spirit, and stared on the mere;
They wished, yet not expected, that they would see
Their dear lord again.
Then the sword began to
Droop, the biting falchion did, from the battle blood,
As icicles melt away. It was one of the wonders
That it all melted down most like ice,
When the Father unlocks the fetter of frost,
Loosens the water-locks—He has the control
Of the shifting seasons: the true Maker He is.
He did not take in that dwelling, the man of the Weather-Geats,
More of the treasures, though he saw many there,
But the head and also the hilt that shone with ornaments.
The sword blade had already melted; the ornamented sword
Had been burnt up, for the blood was hot to such a degree.
The accursed spirit was venomous, who died therein.
Soon the one who had lived through the fight to see the fall
Of the fiends was swimming; he swam through the water upward.
The surging waves had been entirely purged—
The large domain—when the accursed spirit left
The days of living and this world that fleets away.
Then to the land came the seafarers' guardian,
The stouthearted man swam. He was pleased with his booty,
With the heavy load he was carrying with him.
Then they went together, thanked God,
The mighty band of thanes; they rejoiced that

They could see their lord safe and sound again.
Then from the strong one the helmet and the coat of mail
Were removed soon; the lake remained still,
The water under the clouds, stained with blood of the slain.
They marched forth from there with light steps.
Rejoicing in spirit, they measured the path,
The well-acquainted road; the men of kingly bravery
Bore the head from the waterside cliff
With difficulty for each of them,
Valiant though they were. Four of them had to
Carry Grendel's head to the gold-hall
On a shaft of spear, with difficulty,
Until presently to the hall came
The fourteen of the warlike brave Geats.
Among them, the lord of men, in their company,
Walked in high spirit, toward the mead-hall.
Then came in the prince of thanes,
The man daring in deeds, exalted with glory,
The battle-brave hero, to greet Hrothgar.
Then, held by hair, into the hall was brought
Grendel's head, where people were drinking,
Horrifying to the earls, and to the lady, too,
This ghastly sight; people looked on it.
(XXIV) Beowulf spoke, son of Ecgtheow:
"What! Son of Healfdene, lord of the Scyldings,
We are pleased to have brought this booty for you,
As a token of glory that you here now look at.
I, who have scarcely come through it alive,
The fight under the water, ventured on the work
With difficulty: the fight would have been put

To an end right away, had it not been for God's protection.
In the fight I could not accomplish anything
With Hrunting, though that weapon may be a mighty one;
But the Ruler of men granted me
That I saw on the wall an ancient sword hanging,
Beautiful and mighty—most often He has led
The friendless—that I on that cause drew the weapon.
Then I slew the keepers of the house in the fight,
When proper time permitted me. Then the battle-bill,
The ornamented sword, burnt up, as that blood spurted forth—
The hottest of battle blood. I carried that hilt from there,
Away from the fiends: I avenged their atrocious deeds,
Slaughter of the Danes, as it was a proper thing to do.
Then I pledge to you that you may sleep in Heorot,
Free from care with the company of your men,
And each of the thanes of your people may, too,
Your tried warriors and fledglings; that you need not
Fear for them, prince of the Scyldings, on their behalf,
Death of the earls, as you earlier did."
Then the golden hilt was given to the old warrior,
To the hoary war-chief, into his hand,
That ancient work of giants; after the fall of demons,
It passed into the possession of the lord of the Danes,
That wonder-smiths' handiwork; and when the hostile-hearted churl,
That adversary of God, gave up this world,
Guilty of murder, and his mother, too,
It passed into the control of the king of the world,
The best of those between the seas, of those
Who had dispensed treasures in the Danish realm.

Hrothgar spoke—he beheld the hilt,
The time-honored heirloom, on which was engraved
The origin of an ancient strife, when the flood,
The sweeping surges, destroyed the race of giants.
They incurred a terrible result. That was a nation
Estranged from the eternal Lord: for that reason
The Ruler gave them retribution—flood to drown them.
So was on the sword-guard of bright gold
Rightly marked in runic letters, set down and told,
For whom that sword, the best of irons,
Had first been made, its hilt twisted and ornamented
With serpentine figures—
Then the wise man spoke,
Son of Healfdene did—all were silent—:
"Indeed, so may a man say, he who performs truth and justice
To his people and bears in mind all far back—
An old guardian of the land: this earl was
Born to prove better than any! Your glory is exalted
Throughout the distant regions, my friend Beowulf,
Your glory all over the nations. You steadily hold it all,
Your strength with wisdom of mind. I shall fulfill my friendship
To you, as we have recently spoken together. You shall
Truly become a long-lasting solace for your own nation,
And prop for the people. Heremod did not turn out so
For Ecgwela's offspring, for the Honor-Scyldings;[51]
He grew not to be a joy for them, but turned out
Slaughter and destruction for the Danish people;
Enraged, he killed his table companions,
His shoulder-to-shoulder pals, till he became an outcast,

51. Ecgwela must have been a forbear in the Danish royalty, probably even before Scyld Scefing, for Heremod is known to have been a predecessor of Scyld.

A king in glory, yet far away from the joy of mingling
With people, though the mighty God may have exalted him
With the pleasure of power, and advanced him to be over all men.
Yet his heart grew bloodthirsty in spirit toward them.
No rings did he give to the Danes for their glory;
Deprived of joy, he lived on to suffer
Distress of the strife, the long-term affliction
To his people. Let this teach you a lesson,
And understand what manly virtues are. Wise with winters,
I have told this tale for your sake. It is a wonder to say
How the mighty God in his bounteous will
Dispenses wisdom, land, and nobility
To mankind: He owns the power over all.
Sometimes He lets the mind of a man
Of noble birth move in love,
Gives him worldly joy in his homeland,
A stronghold of men as his domain,
Renders regions in the world so subject to his rule,
A large kingdom that he himself cannot conceive
An end to it all, due to his unwiseness.
He lives in prosperity: neither disease nor old age
Hinders him at all, nor a sad thought throws
Dark shadow in his mind, nor hostility anywhere
Breeds a deadly feud, but to him the whole world
Moves along as he wishes; he knows nothing worse—
(XXV) Till in his mind a great deal of arrogance
Grows and flourishes; then the overseer sleeps,
The soul's guardian does. That sleep is too deep,
Bound in its troubles, a slayer very near—
One who from an arrow-bow shoots him unnoticed.

Then is he hit in his heart under the helmet
With the sharp arrow—no way to protect himself—
With the crooked cryptic commands of the accursed spirit;
What he has long held seems trivial to him.
He covets furiously, does not honorably dispense
Ornamented treasures, and he forgets and neglects
His future state, as God, the Lord of glory,
Previously gave him a great deal of honor.
It comes to pass in turn in the end
That the fleeting body declines,
Falls fated; another seizes the earl's
Ancient treasure—one who unsparingly dispenses
The treasures, and does not heed to fear.
Protect yourself against that wickedness, dear Beowulf,
Best of men, and choose the better—
The eternal good counsels; do not indulge in arrogance,
Glorious champion! The glory of your might is here now
Only for a while; soon will it be
That disease or sword will deprive you of strength,
Or fire's swallowing, or flood's surging,
Or sword's attack, or spear's flight,
Or dire old age; or brightness of eyes
Will diminish and grow dim; shortly will it be
That death, warrior, will overpower you.
So I have ruled the Ring-Danes for half of a century
Beneath the clouds, and have protected them in war,
With spears and swords, against many tribes
All over this middle-earth, so that I have thought that
None could be my adversary beneath the sky's expanse.
Alas, reversal of it came to me in my homeland,

Grief after joy, when Grendel appeared—
That old adversary of mine came to invade.
I continually suffered great sorrow of soul for
The devastation he caused. May God, the eternal Lord,
Be thanked, for that I have ever come to experience
That I look on that blood-stained head
With my own eyes, after the old strife!
Go now to your seat, and enjoy the delightful feast,
Distinguished in battle; a great deal of treasures
We shall share, when morning comes."
    The Geat was glad at heart, went soon to
Seek his seat, as the wise man commanded.
Then a feast was fairly prepared again as before,
For the brave men sitting about in the hall,
All over again—
                    A veil of night lowered—
Dark over the warriors; the whole band of retainers arose.
The gray-haired one, the aged Scylding, wished to
Retire in bed. The Geat, the brave shield-warrior,
Was pleased to rest well without measure.
Soon a hall-thane showed forth the way to him,
Weary of venture, coming from a far-off land;
He for courtesy's sake attended to all the needs
Of the thane—such as at that time
The seafaring warriors should have.

[1799–1924: Beowulf prepares for his return to his homeland; Beowulf gives his pledge of lasting friendship to Hrothgar and his son Hrethric, and Hrothgar bids farewell to Beowulf; Beowulf embarks on his journey back to his homeland, and arrives in Geatland.]

Then the big-hearted man rested. The building soared high,
Vaulted and gold-adorned; the guest slept within,
Till the black raven blithe of heart announced
The joy of heaven. Then came the bright beam,
[Light over the shadows]; the warriors hastened,
The nobles were eager to set out to sail
To their people again; the visitor, bold of spirit,
Wished to seek his ship far from there.

Then the brave one bade to bear Hrunting
To the son of Ecglaf,[52] asked him to take back his sword,
His dear iron, thanked him for the favor rendered,
Said that he reckoned it a good battle-companion,
Powerful in war, never in words found fault
With the sword—that was a gracious man.[53]
And then the warriors were eager to depart,
Ready with arms. The prince honored by the Danes
Went to the high seat, where the other was;
The battle-brave warrior greeted Hrothgar.
(XXVI) Beowulf spoke, son of Ecgtheow:
"Now we seafarers coming from far off
Wish to say that we are anxious to
Return to Hygelac. We have been well treated
Here to our desire. You have dealt with us well.
If then on earth I may in any way
Earn more of your heart's love,
Lord of men, than I have done heretofore
With warlike deeds, I should be ready soon.

52. "the son of Ecglaf" is Unferth.

53. Hrunting was not of much help in his fight with Grendel's mother. (See ll. 1518–28.)

If I hear of that beyond the stretch of the sea,
That your neighbors threaten you with terrors,
As your enemies have done in the past,
I will bring a thousand thanes to you,
Men to your aid. I know of Hygelac,
Lord of the Geats, though he is young
To be the guardian of a people, that he will support me
With words and deeds, so that I may honor you well
And bring a forest of spears to your aid,
Augmenting your strength, where you have need of men.
If then Hrethric, your princely son, decides to visit
The court of the Geats, he can find there
Many friends; far countries are even better to seek
For one, who himself is a man of worth."
    Hrothgar spoke to him in answer:
"The Lord in His wisdom sent those words
Into your mind; I have not heard a man
In so young an age speak more wisely.
You are a man of great strength, prudent mind,
And wise words! I consider it likely,
If it happens that spear, sword-fierce battle,
Takes the son of Hrethel,[54]
Sickness or sword seizes your lord,
The guardian of people, and you retain your life,
That the Sea-Geats will not have any man
Better to choose as their king, as guardian of
Their treasure, if you wish to hold the kingdom
That belongs to your kinsmen. Your inner soul has long
Pleased me so well, dear Beowulf.

54. "the son of Hrethel" refers to Hygelac.

You have brought it about that peace shall
Be shared by two nations, people of the Geats
And the Spear-Danes, and strife shall cease,
Hostile acts that they have done so far.
While I rule the wide kingdom, treasures
Shall be shared; many a man shall greet
Another with gifts over the gannet's bath-pool;
The ring-prowed ship will bring over the seas
Gifts and friendly tokens; I know your people
Both with foe and with friend are firmly disposed,
Follow old ways, faultless in every respect."
    And then the protector of earls gave him within,
The son of Healfdene did, twelve treasures.
He bade him to go to his dear people
With the gifts safely, and come again quickly.
Then the good king of noble descent,
The prince of the Scyldings, kissed the best of thanes,
And hugged him by the neck; tears fell from
The gray-haired man: for the wise old man, there was
Expectation of two things, of one of them more,
That they henceforth would not be allowed to see each other
In such bold spirit at meeting. The man was so dear to him
That he could not restrain his heart's welling,
But firmly tied by heart-strings in his bosom,
Hidden longing after the dear man
Burned in his blood.
                    Away from him there Beowulf,
Warrior wearing gold adornment, walked on the grassy earth,
Exulting with his treasure. The ship awaited
Its lordly owner, that rode at anchor.

Then on the way the gift of Hrothgar was
Praised often; that was a peerless king,
Flawless in every way, till age deprived him
Of the joys of strength—age that often injured many.
(XXVII) Then came to the sea the band of
Brave young men; they bore ring-nets,
Interlocked mail-jackets. The coastguard perceived
The return of the warriors, as he had done before;
He did not greet the guests with harsh words
From the cliff's bluff, but rode down toward them,
And said that the warriors in bright armor on their way
To the ship would be welcome to the people of the Geats.
Then on the sand was the sea-spacious ship
Loaded with war-gears, the ring-prowed ship,
With horses and treasures; the mast stood high—
High over Hrothgar's treasures hoarded up.
He gave to the boat-guard a sword bound
In gold, that he thenceforth was the more
Honored at mead-bench for the treasure
He had received. The ship embarked to stir up
The deep water; it left the land of the Danes.
Then on the mast was a sail, the sea-garment
Was fastened by a rope; the ship creaked.
There wind was no hindrance for the ship
To journey over the waves; the ship fared,
Floated, foamy-necked, forth over the wave,
Boat with bound prow over the sea-streams,
Till they could see the cliffs of the Geats,
Familiar headlands. The ship pressed onward,
And, driven by the wind, stood on land to moor.

A sea-guard was swiftly ready at the harbor,
He who had watched out far on the sea
For a long time, eager to receive dear men;
He[55] moored the spacious ship to the sand
Firmly by anchor-ropes, for fear that the force of the waves
Pull the fair wooden vessel away from them.
Then he ordered that the treasure of the nobles be borne,
Ornaments and plated gold; it was not far from there
For them to visit the treasure-dispenser,
Hrethel's son, Hygelac, where at home he dwelt
Close by the sea wall, himself with his retainers.

[1925–2199: A brief eulogy of Hygd, Hygelac's queen, is followed by a digression on the shrewish behavior of Thryth before she became Offa's queen; Beowulf arrives at Hygelac's court, and a banquet is held to celebrate his safe return; Beowulf recounts his venture at Hrothgar's court, and comments on the prospect of Freawaru, Hrothgar's daughter, becoming a peace-maker by marrying Ingeld the Heatho-Bard; Beowulf recounts his fight with Grendel and his mother, and presents Hrothgar's gifts to Hygelac; Hygelac bestows Hrethel's heirloom on Beowulf.]

The building was imposing, the king majestic,
Seated high in the hall. Hygd[56] was very young,

55. "He" refers to Beowulf.

56. Hygd, daughter of Hæreth, is queen of Hygelac. The sudden introduction here of Hygd, followed by the long passage on a shrew-turned-good-wife, even as a digression, is rather out of place. For that reason, some scholars think that a possible scribal error may be an explanation: e.g., "The suddenness of her [Hygd's] introduction here is perhaps due to a faulty text" (Donaldson, *Beowulf*, 33, note). However, one must not forget that one of the characteristics of the poetic sub-genre "epic" is that the poet is at liberty to start telling anything that comes to his mind at any given moment. The preceding sentence was: "The building was imposing, the king majestic, Seated high in the hall." It is only natural for the minstrel to say a few words about the queen sitting next to Hygelac. So the minstrel utters a few words in the vein of complimenting her virtues—which leads

Wise, and well-accomplished, though she, Hæreth's
Daughter, had spent few winters in the enclosure of
The fortress; she was not niggardly, though,
Nor too sparing of gifts, of treasures, for the people
Of the Geats. A good queen of the people,
She kept in mind the temper of Thryth, her cruel deed:
None so brave as to dare to venture,
Among her nearby guards—except her lord—[57]
To cast his eyes on her in daylight,
But would reckon a deadly bond ordained,
Having his wrists twisted: swiftly afterwards
He was fated by the sword, after the arrest—
That a patterned sword had to settle it—
Deadly evil made known. Such is not a queen-like practice
For a woman to follow, though she may be peerless,
That a peace-weaver should deprive a dear man
Of his life on the ground of an unsubstantiated blame.[58]
However, Hemming's kinsman[59] put an end to it;
Ale-drinkers have given another account—
That she practiced less harm to the people,
Fewer evil deeds, when for the first time she happened
To be given, gold-adorned, to the young warrior,
Of noble descent when by her father's counsel

---

to mentioning a case that can function as a foil to enhance the effect of what he has just said: the shrewish and virago-like behavior of another woman who also happened to be a queen-to-be.

57. "her lord" refers to her father, not her husband, because her shrewish behavior manifested itself only until she was married off to Offa as a peace-weaver.

58. These lines do not mean that Thryth persisted with her atrocity of punishing the guiltless even after becoming a queen. What is meant here is that her previous behavior was no longer compatible with her status as a queen after her marriage.

59. "Hemming's kinsman" refers to Offa, king of the Angles. Hemming was a forebear of Offa and his son Eomer.

She sought the hall of Offa on a voyage over
The palely brown billows. There on the throne she,
Afterwards well renowned for her goodness,
Made use of her destined life while living;
She harbored deep love for the prince of warriors—[60]
According to what I have heard, the choicest
Of the whole human race between the seas,
Of mankind, for the reason that Offa was a man
With spear-like bravery with gifts and wars,
Widely honored, and ruled his native land wisely.
From him was born Eomer, who was to be
A prop for warriors—Hemming's kinsman,
Grandson of Garmund, granted with gift in waging wars.[61]
(XXVIII) Then the brave one walked with his band,
Treading on the sand over the plain by the sea,
The wide shore stretched. The world's light-giver shone,
The sun hastened from the south. They made their way,
Anxiously walked to where the protector of earls,
The slayer of Ongentheow,[62] the brave young war-king,
As they had heard say, dealt out the rings
In his stronghold. The coming of Beowulf
Was quickly announced to Hygelac,
That there in his domain the defender of warriors,
His shield-companion, who had come alive
Safe and sound from battle, was approaching the court.

60. "the prince of warriors" refers to Offa, to whom Thryth was married.

61. A case of "the taming of the shrew": Thryth was married to Offa as a peace-maker; she was completely transformed after marrying Offa; she gave birth to Eomer, who was son of Offa and grandson of Garmund—all descending from Hemming.

62. Ongentheow was a Swedish king, whose story is told in Fitts XL and XLI (ll. 2922–98). Hygelac is called the slayer of Ongentheow, for the former led an expedition against the Scylfings (the Swedes), which resulted in the latter's death.

The hall was quickly cleared within, as the mighty
One bade, for the guests to arrive on foot.
Then he who had survived the fight sat with the king,
Kinsman with kinsman, after he greeted his liege lord,
His trusty friend, in ceremonious speech with solemn
Words. Hæreth's daughter[63] moved about
Through that hall-building with mead-bowls,
Genially tended on the people, and bore a jar of drink
To pour for the men. Hygelac began to
Inquire of his companion with courtesy
In the high hall—curiosity pressed hard on him—
What the adventures of the Sea-Geats had been:
"How was your journey, dear Beowulf,
When you suddenly resolved to seek
Battle far off over the salt water,
The fight at Heorot? Did you somehow provide
Remedy for the wide-known woe for Hrothgar,
The renowned prince? I for that was restless in care,
Unable to suppress surging worries, didn't trust
The venture of a dear man; I entreated you long
That you make no attempt to assault the damned spirit,
Let the South-Danes settle for themselves
By waging a fight with Grendel. I thank God
For allowing me to see you sound and safe."
Beowulf spoke, son of Ecgtheow:
"It is not a hidden matter, lord Hygelac,
The big match, for many of the men,
What a time of fight between us two, I and Grendel,
Happened in that place, where he had caused

63. "Hæreth's daughter" is Hygd, queen of Hygelac.

A great many sorrows for the Victory-Scyldings,
Miseries for ever; I avenged that all,
So that any of Grendel's kinsfolk over
The earth need not boast of that din at dawn,
Whoever lives longest of the loathsome race,
Soaked in sin. I first arrived there
At the ring-hall to greet Hrothgar;
Soon the renowned son of Healfdene,
When he knew my intention,
Assigned me a seat his sons might deserve.
The company was in joy; I had never seen till then
Under the heaven-vault a greater mirth over mead
Of those gathered in a hall. Now and again the renowned queen,
Peace-pledge of the people, moved about the entire hall,
Cheering the young men; often she handed
A ring-band to a man, before she went to her seat.
Now and again the daughter of Hrothgar bore
The ale-cup to the retainers, to all the earls, taking turns,
Whom I heard those sitting in the hall
Call Freawaru, when she handed the studded
Bowl to the warriors. She is promised to wed,
Young and gold-adorned, the gracious son of Froda;[64]
The friend of the Scyldings, the guardian of the kingdom,
Has decided on that, and considers it a wise policy
That he settle a great deal of deadly feuds and conflicts
By means of this woman. Hardly in any nation,
After the fall of a prince, the deadly spear rests
Even for a little while, though the bride may be good.
Then it may displease the prince of the Heatho-Bards

64. "son of Froda" is Ingeld the Heatho-Bard, to whom Freawaru, daughter of Hrothgar, is betrothed.

And each of the thanes of that people,
When he, the wedding attendant of the Danes
Nobly feasted, goes into the hall with the woman;
On them will shine the old heirlooms, the hard and
Ring-adorned treasure that belonged to the Heatho-Bards
While they could wield the weapons,[65]
[XXIX–XXX] Till they led to destruction, to war,
Their dear companions' lives and their own selves'.
Then upon seeing the treasure at beer drinking, an old warrior,
The one who remembers all—many a man's death by the spear—
Will speak, grim in his heart full of sorrow—
Will begin to make a trial of a young warrior
In his spirit by imparting the thought in his heart,
To arouse warlike spirit, and will utter this word:
"My friend, can you recognize that sword,
The precious iron, which your father bore to battle
Wearing a warlike mask for the last time,
Where the Danes, the fierce Scyldings, slew him,
And took control of the battle-field,
When Withergyld[66] lay dead, after the fall of the warriors?
Now here the son of a certain one of his slayers
Walks in the hall, exulting with his adornments,
Boasts of the butchery, and bears the treasure
That should have been yours by right."
So will he incite and remind on each occasion
With sore words, till the time comes
That the woman's thane, for his father's deeds,

65. That is, "When the Scyldings, at the wedding of Freawaru and Ingeld, carry the heirlooms that used to belong to the Heatho-Bards, the latter will feel indignant."

66. Withergyld was probably a leader of the Heatho-Bards in their confrontation with the Scyldings.

Receives a sword-blow to fall down blood-stained,
With his life forfeited. The other escapes
From there alive, knows the land well.
Then on both sides, the pledges made by the earls
Will be broken; thereupon deadly hate will well up
In Ingeld, and after the surging of sorrow
The love he feels for his wife will turn cold.
Therefore, I do not consider the loyalty of the Heatho-Bards,
Their share in the alliance with the Danes, free from deceit—
Nor their friendship firmly fixed. I shall speak forth
Further about Grendel, that you may readily know,
Dispenser of treasure, what since came about with
The hand-to-hand grapple of the fighters. When heaven's jewel[67]
Had glided over the grounds, the enraged ghost came,
Ghastly and hostile in the dark, to seek us out,
Where, unharmed, we were guarding the hall.
There the fight was fatal to Hondscio,[68] deadly to him,
For he was one doomed to die. He, an armed warrior,
Was the first one to lie dead; Grendel proved himself
A slayer by gorging, for the glorious young retainer,
For he devoured the entire body of the beloved man.
The slayer with blood-stained teeth, intent on
Devastation, was not ready to leave the gold-hall—
Not quite yet, without a booty grabbed in his hand;
But he, monstrously powerful, attacked me,
And instantly took me in his grip. His glove hung
Wide and eerie, fastened by cunning clasps;

67. "heaven's jewel" is an allusion to the sun.

68. Hondscio: Grendel's first victim on the night of Beowulf's vigil at Heorot; since Beowulf readily mentions his name, he was probably a Geat, one of Beowulf's companions in the venture.

It had been all contrived with ingenuity—
With the devil's devices and the dragon's peels.
He would put me, one of many, therein—
The fierce perpetrator of evil deeds would—
Though guiltless I was. He could not do so,
For I in anger had stood up tall and stalwart.
It is too long to recount how I paid back
To the folk-ravager what's due for his evil deeds.
I have done honor to your nation, my prince,
By doing what I did there. He escaped away—
Only to brook the joy of life a little while.
However, his right hand remained behind
In Heorot, and he, crest-fallen, from there,
Sad of heart, sank to the floor of the mere.
The lord of the Scyldings rewarded me
For the deadly fight greatly with plated gold,
With many treasures, when morning came
And we sat down for a feast.
There was song and jubilee; the old Scylding,[69]
Informed well, told tales from far-off times.
Now and again the battle-brave one strummed the harp,
Partook of the joy in the mirthful wood, to tell
Sometimes a tale true and sad, sometimes a strange story—
The great-hearted king recounted in a rightful manner;
At times, again, fettered with age,
The old warrior began to lament the lapse of his youth,
His martial prowess; his heart surged within, as he

69. "the old Scylding" can mean either "the old Dane" or "an old Dane," depending on the context. If we choose the former, it refers to Hrothgar; if the latter, someone other than Hrothgar. But since the phrase "the great-hearted king" appears soon (l. 2110), we may as well take it as alluding to Hrothgar. For that reason, I take "the battle-brave one" (l. 2107) as alluding to Hrothgar also.

Recalled many a thing from the winters he had lived.
Thus we took pleasure therein the entire day,
Till another night came back to men.
Then Grendel's mother in her turn was
Swiftly ready to revenge the injuries done,
Made a journey, mortified; death had taken her son,
Martial hate of the Weather-Geats had.
The female monster avenged her brat:
Brutally she butchered a warrior; that was
Æschere, wise old counselor deprived of life.
When morning came, they could not, the people
Of the Danes could not, burn him, death-weary,
In the fire, nor could they put on a pyre
Their beloved man: she had borne off his body
In her fiendish embrace down into a mountain-stream.
That was for Hrothgar the most painful of sorrows,
Which had long befallen the people's guardian.
Then the prince, troubled in heart, entreated me,
For the sake of your name, to perform a heroic deed,
Risk my life, and fulfill a glorious achievement,
In the watery tumult; he promised me reward.
Then I found the keeper of the abysmal deep
That is widely known, the grim and horrid one.
There between us two was hand-grapple awhile.
Water bubbled with blood, and in that battle-hall
I severed the head of Grendel's mother
With a mighty sword. Barely from there
I bore away my life; I was not then doomed to die yet,
But the protector of earls bestowed on me again
A great many treasures, Healfdene's son did.

(XXXI) So the people's king lived in good customs.
I had not lost the gifts at all, the reward of my strength,
But he gave me treasures—Healfdene's son did—
In accordance with what I myself deemed suitable.
I will bring these to you, my brave king,
And present them gladly. All is still
Dependent on your favor; I have few
Close kinsmen, except you, Hygelac."

Then he ordered to bring in the boar-head banner,
The helmet towering in battle, the gray mail-shirt,
The splendid sword, and then spoke thus:
"Hrothgar gave this battle-wear to me,
The wise king did; he commanded emphatically
That I should first tell you about this gift;
He said that King Heorogar[70] had kept it,
Lord of the Scyldings had, for a long time;
Not so readily would he[71] have given the breast-wear
To his son, bold Heoroweard,[72] although he had been
Loyal to his father. Enjoy it all well!"

I have heard that four swift-paced horses followed
The treasures, alike all in apple-fallow;
He made a gift to him of both—
The horses and the treasures; so must kinsmen act,
Must never weave the net of malice for each other
With hidden craft, or plot for the deaths of
Close companions. To Hygelac was his nephew
Very trust-worthy for his hardiness at battles,
And each to the other was mindful of being helpful.

70. Heorogar was Hrothgar's elder brother and the first son of Healfdene.

71. That is, Heorogar.

72. Heoroweard was son of Heorogar, therefore, Hrothgar's nephew.

I have heard that he gave the neck-ring—the splendid
Jewel of wonder Wealhtheow had given him—
To Hygd, a prince's daughter, along with three horses,
Graceful and saddle-bright; since then her breast
Was adorned with the ring she received then.

Thus the son of Ecgtheow proved himself valiant.
A man with warlike fame and praised for brave deeds,
He acted in pursuit of glory. He never slew drunken
Hearth-companions;[73] his temper was not fierce,
But he, brave in battle, with the greatest strength
Among mankind, kept the bounteous gift that
God had granted him. He had long been of low esteem;
So the Geatish people did not consider him much of a man,
Nor would the lord of the Weathers make him
Entitled to much merit-mark on the mead bench.
They very much thought that he was a sluggard—feeble
Though born a prince. Change came to the man of glory
For each of the afflictions he had to go through.

Then the guardian of the earls, the battle-brave king,
Ordered to bring in the heirloom of Hrethel[74]
Bedecked with gold; for the Geats then
There was no finer treasure in the shape of a sword.
He laid that down on Beowulf's lap,
And gave him seven thousand [hides of land],
A hall, and a princely seat. To both of them alike
Land had been bequeathed as inborn right in the country,
The ancestral domain, though for the other more

73. E. Talbot Donaldson's prose translation reads, "Drunk, he slew no hearth-companions." But as the manuscript reads 'druncne'—a word in accusative-plural form—it means; "[he] never slew drunken hearth-companions."

74. Hrethel was Hygelac's father.

Expansive was the realm, for he was higher in status.

[2200–2323: Beowulf succeeds the throne after the deaths of Hygelac and his son Heardred, and reigns peacefully for fifty years; a fire-spewing dragon devastates the land in revenge for its hoard stolen.]

It happened afterwards in later days that,
When Hygelac lay slain in the clashes of battle,
And the battle-swords became the bane
Of Heardred[75] under the shield-covering—
When the War-Scylfings, the hardy warriors,
Sought him out in the victorious people
And fiercely attacked Hereric's nephew—[76]
Then to Beowulf was the wide realm
Passed on for reign. He ruled well
For fifty winters—he was a wise king,
An old guardian of the land—till a certain creature,
A dragon, began to hold sway in the dark nights,
Which had kept watch over a hoard on the high heath,
A steep stone-barrow. A path lay underneath,
Unknown to men. Thereon went in
One of the human species, one who made his way
To the heathen hoard; his hand took a large cup,
A shining treasure. He could not hide it thereafter,
Though sleeping, the dragon happened to be tricked
By the thief's treachery, for the people found out—
Those dwelling near did—, that he was enraged.
(XXXII) He who sorely injured the dragon did not break

75. Heardred was Hygelac's son, who succeeded his father as king of the Geats. The occasion of his death is narrated later, in Fitt XXXIII (ll. 2379b–90).

76. Hereric was Hygd's brother, hence Heardred's maternal uncle.

Into the serpent's hoard of his own accord, on his own will,
But for dire distress: the slave of someone of
The children of men fled hateful blows,
In need of a refuge, and made his way therein,
The man burdened with guilt. [. . . . .
. . . .
. . . .
. . . .
. . . .
. . . .][77] There was a great deal of
Such ancient treasures in that earth-cave,
As in the olden days a certain one of mankind
Had thoughtfully hidden them there,
An enormous legacy of a noble race,
The precious treasures. Death had taken them all
In bygone days, and the only one still alive,
Of the clansmen, he had stirred there longest,
Guardian mourning after friends; he expected the same—
That he would be able to enjoy the ancient treasure
Not for a long while. A mound fully prepared
Stood on the plain near the sea-waves, newly built
By the headland, and fixed by an art of forbidding access.
Thereto the keeper of the rings bore in a portion of
The earls' treasures worth to be hoarded—plated gold.
Then he spoke a few words:
    "Hold now, you earth, the heroes' property,
Now men may not! What, good men obtained it,
First from you. War-death, the dreadful deadly evil,
Has carried off every one of my men, of my people;

77. Since the manuscript is in such a state of ruin, I did not intend to put the lines into something that makes any sense.

Each has left this life, of those who have seen the hall-joy.
I do not have anyone who would carry my sword
Or would polish my ornamented flagon,
My dear drinking bowl. All the retainers are gone elsewhere.
The strong helmet must remain bereft of fair-wrought ornament,
Of its gold plates: the burnishing men sleep in death,
Who should polish the battle mask that it may shine.
And also the mail-coat, which at war lived through
The clashing of shields and the cutting of swords,
Decays after the warrior; the ring-mail cannot
Journey with the battle-leader going far away,
Shoulder to shoulder with his warriors. There is no joy
Of a harp, no delight in the glee-wood; nor does a good hawk
Fly through the hall, nor do a swift horse's pounding hooves
Beat the courtyard to resound. Baleful death has
Sent forth many of the living men!"

Thus, sad of thought, he uttered words of sorrow,
The one left alone after all were gone, moved about
Joyless day and night, till the surging of death
Touched his heart. The old depredator-at-dawn
Found the delightful treasures stand open,
The one who, while burning, seeks barrows,
The naked malevolent dragon that flies by night,
Enwrapped in fire; the land-dwellers
Dread him dearly. He is wont to visit
The hoard in the earth, where he, grown wary over the winters,
Guards the heathen gold—a task bringing no benefit.

Thus for three hundred years the people's ravager
Had occupied in the earth one of the treasure-houses,
Magnificently large, till one man made his heart

Inflamed with rage: he bore to his master
A gold-plated flagon, and pleaded to his lord
For peaceful pardon. Then was the hoard explored,
The hoard of rings diminished, the petition granted
To the poor man: his lord cast his eyes on
The ancient work of men, for the first time.

When the serpent awoke, the strife was renewed.
Then he[78] swiftly moved along a rock, and, hard-hearted,
Found his foe's foot-track; he[79] had footed forward
In stealthy steps too close to the dragon's head.
So may a man not doomed yet easily come through
His woe and exile—he who is guarded
By God's grace! The hoard's guardian searched
Eagerly along the ground: he wished to find the man,
Who had dealt with him unfairly while he was asleep.
Hot and fierce in mood, he often moved about
All outside the mound—there was no man to be found
In the wilderness; however, he rejoiced at rampage,
The act of waging war. At times he turned to the barrow,
And searched for the precious cup; he soon found out
That a certain man had tampered with his gold,
The splendid treasure. The hoard-watcher waited
Impatiently till the evening came.
Then the warden of the barrow became enraged,
The hostile foe wished to pay back with flame for
The dear drinking-bowl lost. Then the day was gone,
To the joy of the serpent: he would not wait long
On the wall, but went forth with fire,

78. "he" refers to the dragon.

79. "he" refers to the thief.

Prepared with flame. The beginning was terrifying
To the people of the land, as it was forthwith to lead
To a grievous end brought upon their treasure-giver.
(XXXIII) Then the stranger began to spew flame
And burn the bright houses—the glow of fire shone forth
To the horror of men; the loathsome flier
Would never leave anything to remain alive there.
The assault of the serpent was seen far and wide,
The malicious marauding from near and from afar,
How much the fight-monger hated and humiliated
The people of the Geats. He hastened again to his hoard,
His hidden hall of splendor, before daylight broke.
He had entrapped the people of the land in flame,
With fire and burning: he had trust in his barrow,
His valor, and the wall; his faith failed him.

[2324–2400: Beowulf prepares himself for a fight with the dragon; there follows a retrospective account of the war in which Hygelac met his death and the ensuing events involving the death of Heardred, Hygelac's son, and Beowulf's inheriting the throne of Geatland.]

Then the horror was made known to Beowulf
Straightaway in truth—that his own dwelling,
The best of buildings, the gift-seat of the Geats,
Had melted in the surge of fire. That was distress in heart
To the good man, the greatest sadness within;
The wise man thought that he might have
Bitterly offended the Ruler, the eternal Lord,
By a breach of the old law: his breast surged within
With gloomy thoughts, as was unusual to him.

The fire-dragon had destroyed the stronghold of people,
The shoreline land without, the fortress itself
With flames; for that the warrior-king,
The prince of the Weather-Geats, planned to punish him.
    Then the protector of the warriors, the lord of earls,
Ordered them to make a wondrous shield,
Entirely of iron: he readily knew
That wood from forest, a linden shield, could not
Help him against fire. The non-paralleled prince
Was bound to live to see the end of the transitory days,
Of worldly life—and the serpent also, though
He had long guarded the hoard of wealth.
Then the king of rings scorned to make an assault
At the far-reaching flier with a flock of men,
A bulky band; he did not fear a battle for himself,
And did not make much out of the war-faring of the serpent,
His strength and valor, because he had previously
Gone through many battles, venturing on difficulty,
The clashes of war, since the time when he, a man
Blessed with victory, had purged the hall of Hrothgar,
And at a fight had crushed the clan of Grendel
Of the hateful line.
                    Nor was that the smallest
Of his close combats, in which Hygelac was slain,
When the king of the Geats, people's lord and friend,
Son of Hrethel, died in the storm of a battle,
In Friesland, in a falchion-biting fight,
Struck by a sword. From there Beowulf came
By his sheer strength, crossing the strokes of the waves;
He had on his arm the battle-gear of thirty

Of his opponents, when he set out to the sea.
The Hetware[80] had no cause to be exultant in
The battle on foot, those who bore their shields
In front, against him; few came back alive again
From that warrior, and returned to their homes.
Then Ecgtheow's son swam across the watery expanse,[81]
A forlorn solitary man, back to his people;
Then Hygd offered him treasure and the kingdom,
Rings and the royal seat: she had no faith in her son—
That he would be able to maintain the ancestral thrones
Against foreign troops, now that Hygelac was dead.
Yet the poor lordless people could not prevail
Upon the princely nobleman by any means
That he would consent to be lord to Heardred,
Or that he would accept the kingly power.[82]
But he upheld Heardred among people by friendly counsel,
With good will built on honor, till the latter grew older
And ruled the Weather-Geats.
The exiled men sought
Heardred across the sea, the sons of Ohthere[83] did.
They had rebelled against the protector of the Scylfings,[84]
The mightiest of the sea kings that dispensed
Treasure in the land of the Swedes—a renowned prince.

80. The Hetware was a Frankish tribe allied to the Frisians in their fight against the Geats.

81. The word "oferswam" literally means "swam over"; it can also figuratively mean "sailed across," not by physical swimming, but on a vessel.

82. I.e., The Geats could not persuade Beowulf to be their king after Hygelac's death, for he would not bypass Heardred, son of Hygelac and legitimate heir to the throne.

83. "the sons of Ohthere" is an allusion to Eanmund and Eadgilds, whose right to the Swedish throne, after their father's death, was taken away by their usurping uncle, Onela, Ohthere's bother.

84. "the protector of the Scylfings" refers to Onela.

To Heardred that happened to mark the end of his life;
For his hospitality there he received a mortal wound,
Hygelac's son did, by the strokes of a sword.
And the son of Ongentheow[85] departed again
To seek his home after Heardred lay dead,
Leaving Beowulf behind to sit on the royal seat
And rule the Geats. That was a good king!
(XXXIV) He kept in mind requital for the calamity
In later days, and became a friend to
The all-bereft Eadgils; with his people he supported
The son of Ohthere[86] over the wide sea,
With warriors and weapons; he avenged afterwards
By a bitter careworn expedition, and took the king's life.[87]
Thus he had survived each of the battles,
The fierce combats, the son of Ecgtheow had,
Of the works of valor, till that one day,
On which he had to fight with the serpent.

[2401–2509: Beowulf arrives at the dragon's cave with eleven warriors and a guide; Beowulf reminisces his upbringing in Hrethel's guardianship, Hrethel's grief over the loss of his first son, Herebeald, killed accidentally by his brother Hæthcyn, the feud between the Swedes and the Geats after Hrethel's death,

85. "the son of Ongentheow" refers to Onela.

86 "the son of Ohthere" refers to Eadgils.

87. The brief digression on the occasion of Heardred's death and Beowulf's revenge for his death follows this story line: Ohthere succeeded his father Ongentheow as king of the Scylfings. Upon Ohthere's death his brother Onela seized the throne, thereby forcing Ohthere's sons, Eanmund and Eadgils, to take refuge at the court of Heardred. On account of the favor Heardred bestowed on the two princes put in exile, Onela attacked him; and in the ensuing battle both Heardred and Eanmund were killed. When his intended chastisement on Heardred for protecting Ohthere's sons was fulfilled, Onela returned to Sweden, leaving Geatland to be in the care of Beowulf. Beowulf looked after Eadgils, the surviving son of Ohthere, and helped him reclaim kingship of Sweden after slaying the usurper Onela.

and how all his life he has been loyal to the throne and the people of his nation.]

Then, aroused to anger, the lord of the Geats—
One of twelve—went to look upon the dragon.
He had then learnt from where the disaster arose,.
The dire affliction of men: the renowned treasure cup,
Through the informer's hand, had come to his possession.
He was the thirteenth man in the troop—
The one who had brought about the beginning of the broil;
The sad slave, the wretched one, had to from there
Show the way to the place. Against his wish he went
To where he knew a certain earth-hall—
The cave under the ground near the sea-surge,
The tossing waves; within, it was overflowing
With ornaments and fineries. The dreadful guard,
The alert fighter, old under the earth,
Kept the golden treasures. That was not an object
That any man could attain in an easy bargain.
Then on the headland sat the battle-brave king,
While the prince of the Geats wished good luck for
His hearth-companions. He was sad in heart,
Uneasy, yet ready for death, the fate being so near
That should come upon the old man,
Try to reach the hoard of soul, and part asunder
Life from the body; not for long afterwards
The prince's life was enclosed in flesh.
Beowulf spoke, son of Ecgtheow:
"In youth I survived many of the battle-storms,
Of the times of war—I remember that all.

I was seven years old, when the prince of the rings—
The friendly lord of the people—took me from my father:
King Hrethel took charge of me and kept me,
Gave me treasure and feast, remembered our kinship;
In his lifetime I was never any less dear to him
As a man at arms in his stronghold than any of his sons—
Herebeald, Hæthcyn, or Hygelac, my dear lord.
For the eldest a violent death-bed was spread
Inappropriately by the deeds of a kinsman—
When Hæthcyn struck him down, his friendly lord,
With an arrow shot from his horn-bow,
Missed the mark, and shot his kinsman dead—
One brother killed another, with the bloody arrow-shaft.
That was a fight inexpiable, unfortunately perpetrated,
Wearying to the heart; yet so did it happen, no matter
How a prince had to lose his life without being avenged.
So heart chilling it is for a hoary man
To endure that his son should swing so young
Upon the hanging gallows; then he may utter a dirge,
A mournful song, when his son is hanging
For the joy of the raven, and he cannot perform
Any help to him, though himself old and wise.
The death of his son is incessantly remembered
Upon each sunrise; he does not care to
Wait for another heir to succeed in his
Stronghold, when the one, through the mandate
Of death, has undergone all experiences.
The sorrowful man sees in his son's dwelling
A wine-hall wasted, a windy bedroom
Deprived of joy—the riders sleep,

The warriors in the grave; no sound of the harp,
No joy in the dwelling is there, as there were before.
(XXXV) He then goes to bed, and sings a song of sorrow—
A man longing for a man;[88] the fields and the homestead—
All seemed hollow to him. Thus the protector
Of the Weather-Geats bore in his heart grief
Welling after Herebeald; he could by no means
Settle the feud by retribution on the slayer;
None the sooner could he chastise the warrior[89]
For his hateful deeds, though he was not dear to him.
Then with the grief that had befallen him too bitterly
He gave up joy among men, and chose God's light:
He left for his sons land and towns, as does
A prosperous man, when he departed from life.
Then there was hostility and strife between Swedes and Geats
Across the wide water, a feud affecting both sides,
A severe belligerent enmity, when Hrethel died.
And the sons of Ongentheow[90] were
Bold and battle-brave, and did not wish to maintain
Friendship over the seas; but around Hreosnabeorh[91]
They often perpetrated dire malicious slaughter.
That my kinsmen redressed with vengeance,

88. George Jack (*Beowulf: A Student Edition*, 171, note) gave the following interpretation: "'he chants one song of grief after another' (rather than 'one man chants a song of grief for the other')." Singing one song after another? Hrethel's agony is that he has lost his firstborn, whom he hoped would succeed him in time as king of the Geats. Here we must detect why the poet repeats the same word, "ān" and "ānum": the mourner identifies himself with the one he mourns for.

89. "the warrior" refers to Hæthcyn, who accidentally killed his older brother Herebeald.

90. "the sons of Ongentheow" are Ohthere, who succeeded Ongentheow as king of the Scylfings, and Onela, who usurped the throne after Ohthere's death. See ll. 2379b–96 and the above note relevant to the lines.

91. Hreosnabeorh is a hill in Geatland.

The hostile deed and crime, as it was well-known,
Though one of them paid with his life,
A dear cost; the war turned out fatal
For Hæthcyn, the lord of the Geats.[92]
Then I have heard one kinsman[93] in the morning
Avenged the other[94] on the slayer with the edge of a sword,
When Ongentheow attacked Eofor;[95]
The battle-helm split, the old Scylfing
Fell mortally wounded; his[96] hand remembered
Numerous feuds, and did not withhold deadly blow.
With my shining sword I have repaid
At battle those treasures that he[97] gave me,
As was granted me by fate; he gave me land,
The joy of estate bequeathed. There was no need
For him to seek a warrior with less worth
From among the Gifthas[98] or the Spear-Danes
Or the Swedes, and buy him with treasure;
I would always march ahead of him in his troop,
Alone in the front, and thus throughout my life shall
Fulfill my task at battle, while this sword holds out,
That at all times has never failed to serve me,
Since I in the presence of the troops became

92. Hæthcyn, Hrethel's second son, succeeded his father as king of the Geats, for Herebeald, Hrethel's firstborn, had been killed by an accident. Upon Hæthcyn's death in the battle with the Swedes, Hygelac, his younger brother, became the next king, who, as the ensuing passage indicates, avenged Hæthcyn's death by slaying Ongentheow. Ongentheow's death is narrated in Fitts XL and XLI (ll. 2922–98).

93. "one kinsman" refers to Hygelac.

94. "the other" refers to Hæthcyn.

95. Eofor was a Geatish man who slew Ongentheow.

96 That is, "Eofor's."

97. That is, Hygelac.

98. The Gifthas ("Gifðas") were an East Germanic tribe.

The hand-slayer of Dæghrefn,[99] the Frankish champion—
He could not bring the adornments,.
The breast-ornament, to the king of the Frisians,
But in the battle fell down, keeper of the banner,
A valorous prince; nor was he slain by my sword,
But my fierce handgrip crushed his pulsating heart—
The flesh covering his bones; now shall the sharp blade,
Hand, and a strong sword do the battle to get the hoard."

[2510–2599a: Beowulf speaks to his retainers to declare his resolution to confront the dragon all by himself; Beowulf fights the dragon.]

Beowulf spoke, spoke in words full of boast
For the last time: "I ventured upon many a
Battle in my youthful days; still shall I,
An old guardian of the folk, be glad to fight
To attain a glorious feat, if a heinous ravager
Come out of the earth-hall to confront me."
Then he greeted each of the men,
The bold helmet-wearers for the last time,
His dear companions: "I would not bear a sword,
A weapon, to the worm, if I knew how I could
Otherwise against the fierce foe fulfilling devastation
Grapple with pledge, as I did with Grendel long ago.
But I expect here the hot-burning battle-flame,
Harsh breath and venomous air; that is why I carry
This shield, this coat of mail. I will not flee a step
From the barrow's ward, but it shall for us both henceforth

99. "Day-raven" was a warrior of the Hugas (the Franks), who slew Hygelac and came to be slain by Beowulf.

Happen on the wall as fate dictates for us—
That governs each man's life. My resolution is such that
I scorn to utter an oath against the winged foe.
Wait on the barrow, well protected by your mail-coats,
You, men at arms—to find which of us can better
Endure the wounds inflicted in the deadly encounter
Between the two of us: this is not your undertaking,
Nor is it fitting for any man except me alone,
That he should exert his strength against the monster,
Fulfill a man's job. With valor I shall
Obtain wealth, or war—dire destroyer of life—will
Take your lord away from you!"
    Then the brave warrior up rose by his shield.
Hardy under helmet, he bore his battle-wear
Under the stone-cliffs, trusting the strength
Of one man: such is not what a coward can do!
Then by the wall he saw—he who had come through
Many a battle, brave with manly virtues,
Battle-clashes when the bands on foot beat together—
A stone-arch standing, from where a stream
Bursting out of the barrow; there was surging of a flow,
Hot with deadly flame. He could not
Stay unburned by the dragon's flame
Even for a while at the cave near the hoard.
Swollen with rage, the man of the Weather-Geats
Then let a word burst out of his breast—
Strong-hearted, he shouted. His voice rang clear in battle,
And it resounded in under the gray stone.
Hate was aroused; the hoard's ward knew that
It was man's speech. There was no more time to

Ask for appeasement. First came forth
The breath of the fierce ravager out of the stone,
The burning battle-fume; the earth rumbled.
The man under the barrow, the lord of the Geats,
Swung his shield's rim against the detestable stranger;
Then the heart of the coiled creature was aroused
To burn after battle. The good warrior-king
Had drawn his sword, an ancient heirloom,
Not dull of edge. For each of them was terror
From the other, each being intent on destroying the other.
Stout-hearted stood he with his shield aloft,
The lord of friends, when the serpent swiftly coiled
Its whole body; he waited in full preparation.
Then, burning in flame, it went gliding coiled,
Hastening to its fate. The shield well protected
The life and body of the renowned prince
For a while, but not long as he had purported.
There, for the first time in the days of his life,
He could not assert his claim for triumph at battle,
As fate's decree was not so. The lord of the Geats
Uplifted his hand, struck the multi-colored beast
With his mighty heirloom, that the blade failed,
Gleaming on the bone, bit not so thoroughly
As the king of the folk had need for it,
Oppressed by an ordeal.
Then the barrow's ward
Was in a fierce spirit after the battle-stroke, and
Spewed deadly fire; the battle-flames
Spread wide. The gold-giving friend of the Geats
Boasted of no glorious feat; the battle-sword, drawn

For fight, had failed—as it should never have,
Iron good all the way till then. Nor was that an easy journey,
One that the renowned son of Ecgtheow would
Be willing to take to give up his tie to the land.
He, against his wish, had to take up a dwelling-place
Elsewhere, as each man must depart, leaving his
Fleeting days behind. It was not long till
The two mighty opponents met together again.
The hoard's ward took heart, his heart heaved in breathing,
Once again. Surrounded by flames, he who had once
Ruled a nation came to suffer hard-to-endure pain.
Not at all did the co-fighters of his—
Those sons of the nobles—stand around him in band
With warlike valor; but they fled to the wood,
And saved their lives.

[2599b–2711a: Wiglaf comes to the aid of Beowulf with an heirloom that he has inherited from his father, Weohstan; Wiglaf addresses his companions on the loyalty that a thane owes to his lord; Beowulf dispatches the dragon with the help of Wiglaf.]

Among them all, there was one
Who felt a surge of grief in his heart: a man can never
Annul the ties of kinship, if he is one who thinks rightly.
(XXXVI) His name was Wiglaf, son of Weohstan,
An admirable shield-warrior, a man of the Scylfings,
A kinsman of Ælfhere.[100] He saw his liege lord

100. Nothing is known about Ælfhere besides that he was Wiglaf's kinsman; but as Weohstan is introduced as being of Swedish stock (ll. 2602–3), he was probably one of the Scylfings who fought, as Weohstan did, for Onela in his assault on the Geats—an episode narrated previously (ll. 2379b–96) and in the passage that follows later (ll. 2611–19).

Suffer from heat, under his battle-mask.
He then remembered what property he had given him before,
The rich dwelling-place of the Wægmundings,[101]
Each of the folk-rights, such as his father had possessed.
He could not then hold himself; his hand gripped his shield,
The brown linden, and he drew his time-honored sword.
That was, as known to men, an heirloom of Eanmund,
Ohthere's son, whom—a friendless exile—
Weohstan happened to slay at battle
With his sword's edge, thereafter carrying to his kinsmen
The shining helmet, the ringed mail-coat,
And the old sword giants made. Onela gave it to him,
And the battle-garments of his kinsman,
Ready battle-gear; he did not speak about the feud,
Despite that he had killed the son of his own brother.[102]
He kept the battle-gear for many half-years,
Sword and mail-shirt, till his son could
Attain warriorhood, as his old father had done.
Then he gave him among the Geats every single piece
Of the battle-gear, when he was about to leave life behind,
An old man on his way forth. That was the first time for
The young warrior to partake in the storm of battle,
Shoulder to shoulder with his noble lord.

101. "The Wægmundings" is the appellation for the family to which Beowulf belonged. Later in the poem, Beowulf calls Wiglaf the last of the Wægmundings (ll. 2813–14); but it is not fully explained how Weohstan and Wiglaf, who had Swedish origin, could be of the Wægmundings of the Geats.

102. Weohstan, fighting for Onela in the latter's assault on the Geats for protecting the two sons of Ohthere, his older brother, happened to slay Eanmund, Ohthere's older son, during the battle. Eanmund's battle-gear, including his sword, was presented to Onela as the booty of Weohstan's victory over Eanmund. Onela, knowing that Weohstan had killed his own brother's son, bestowed the heirloom on Weohstan. (Cf. ll. 2379b–96 and the note on those lines above.)

His spirit did not melt, nor did his father's heirloom
Fail at war; the serpent perceived that, when
They had come to confront each other in strife.
    Wiglaf spoke, addressed his companions
With many words of truth—he was sad at heart—:
"I remember that time, when we drank mead.
On such an occasion we pledged to our lord
In the beer-hall, who gave us the rings,
That we would repay him with our battle-gears,
With helmet and hard sword, if such a need should
Befall him. For this reason he chose us from his army
For this expedition by the will of his own,
Took us worthy of glory, and gave me these treasures,
For he considered us to be good spear-wielders,
Brave helmet-wearers—although our lord,
People's guardian, intended to perform
The work of glory all by himself, for he had attained
The foremost feats of glory among men—the greatest
Of all daring deeds. Now is the day come that
Our liege lord is in need of the strength of
Good warriors. Let us go where we should,
To help our battle-leader, though heat there may be—
The grim horror of fire. God knows, as for me,
That I would rather choose to let my body
Be engulfed in flame with my ring-giver.
It does not seem right that we bear our shields
Back to home, unless we first could
Finish off this foe, and protect the life
Of the prince of the Geats. I know well
That his past deeds do not warrant that he must

Suffer affliction all alone among the Geatish host,
And fall in battle. We shall share sword and helmet,
Mail-coat and battle-gear, for common use among us."

Then he waded through the stifling smoke, wearing
A helmet, to help his lord, and spoke, sparing words:
"Dear Beowulf, carry out all well—
So said you long ago in your youth,
That you would not, while you are alive,
Let glory decline. Now, strong-willed prince,
Brave in deeds, you must defend your life
In all your strength; I shall help you."

When these words were over, the wrathful ward came,
The horrid foe in malevolence, a second time,
To attack his enemies, the hated men, all flashing
In a surge of flame. The streak of fire fared forth,
Burnt the shield down to the boss; the battle-shirt
Could not lend any help to the young spear-fighter,
But the young man slid secure and bold
Under his kinsman's shield, when his own was
Burnt down by the flame. Then the warrior-king
Rekindled his zeal for glory, let his battle-sword
Cleave in strong sweep, that it got stuck on the head,
Bearing the heat of his hate. Nægling[103] broke—
The sword of Beowulf failed at battle,
Time-honored and gray with age: it was not granted
That the blades of iron-made swords could be of
Any help to him at battle; his hand was too strong,
The hand that, as I have heard, surpassed any sword
In its stroke, even when he bore to battle
A weapon hardened with wounds: he was no better off for it.

103. Nægling is Beowulf's sword.

Then, for the third time, the ravager of people,
The fearsome fire-dragon, intent on devilish devastation,
Rushed upon the valiant one, when it was given a chance,
Hot and full of hatred. It took his entire neck in the grip
Of its piercing teeth; he turned bloody all over
With the stream of life's water flowing down in flood.
(XXXVII) Then, I have heard, in the presence of his king's need,
The warrior proved his valorous zeal, standing beside his lord,
With his strength and bravery he was born with.
He didn't care about his head, but the hand of the brave
Man got burnt while he was helping his kinsman,
That he struck the malevolent foe somewhat lower,
The man at arms did, so that the sword sank in,
Shining and adorned, that the fire began to
Subside henceforth. Then the king himself still
Had control of his senses, drew his deadly dagger,
Biting and battle-sharp, which he carried on his war-coat;
The guardian of the Geats cut through the worm in the middle.
They had felled their foe—their valor had driven out its life—
And they both together had quelled it down,
The noble kinsmen had. Such should a man be—
A thane at need should. That was for the prince
The last of the victories he had attained by his deeds—
Work in the world.

[2711b–2820: Beowulf recounts to Wiglaf his rule of the Geats before his impending death; Wiglaf brings out some of the dragon's hoard from the cave at Beowulf's bidding; Beowulf gives his last words to Wiglaf.]

Then the wound, which
The earth-dragon had inflicted on him earlier,
Began to burn and swell; he soon found it out
That in his breast, deep inside, venom was welling up
With fierce rage. Then the wise prince walked
To sit down on a seat near the wall;
He looked on the giants' work—
How the ancient earth dwelling had held within
The stone-arches firmly secured by the columns.
Then the thane, boundlessly good, with his hand
Washed the renowned prince, besmeared with blood—
His friend and dear lord, wearied out in battle—,
With water, and untied his helmet.
Beowulf spoke—uttered words despite the wound,
The uncurable cut; he knew all too well
That he had passed through all his days of life,
His earthly joy; when the whole number of days
Had been exhausted, death was to be imminent:
"Now I would have given to my son
My battle-gear, had such been granted me—
An heir who would live on afterwards
With fleshly legacy. I have ruled my people
For fifty winters: there was no folk-king,
None among those of the neighboring peoples,
Who dared to challenge me with his battle forces,
Or threaten with fear. I have waited on this land
For the dictum of destiny, kept my share properly,
Sought no crafty dealings, nor have sworn for my sake
Many oaths wrongfully. In all of this I, though
Weakened with mortal wounds, can have joy;

For there is no cause for the Lord of men to blame me
For slaughter of kinsmen, when life passes away
From my body. Go you now forthwith,
Have a look at the hoard under the gray stone,
Dear Wiglaf, now the serpent is sprawled dead,
Sleeps sorely wounded, deprived of treasure.
Be now in haste, that I may see the ancient riches,
The golden treasure, and clearly examine
The bright jewels finely wrought, so I may,
With more comfort at the abundance of treasure,
Leave my life and my people, whom I have ruled long."
(XXXVIII) Then, I have heard, the son of Weohstan,
Upon hearing these words, quickly obeyed his lord,
Wounded and wearied in battle, and bore his ring-net,
His woven battle-shirt, beneath the roof of the barrow.
Then the victorious one saw, when he went near a seat,
The brave young thane did, many of the precious jewels,
Gold glittering on the ground strewn all over,
Wondrous things on the wall, and the den of the serpent,
Of the old pre-dawn flier, and the cups standing,
The vessels of the men of old, remaining unpolished,
Stripped of their adornments. There was many a helmet
Old and rusty, a multitude of arm-coverings
Skillfully twisted.—Treasure can easily overpower
Anyone of mankind, gold in the ground can,
No matter who may wish to hide it.—
Also he saw a banner wrought of gold
Hanging high over the hoard, the most wondrous work
Woven by handcraft; from it light shone forth,
So that he could see the surface of the floor,

Detect every ornate thing thereon. No trace of the dragon
Was to be seen there, for a sword had carried him off.
Then, I have heard, the sole man plundered
The hoard, the old work of the giants in the barrow;
He heaped up cups and plates on his lap
Upon his choice; he also took the banner—
The brightest of beacons. His old lord's sword—
Its blade was of iron—earlier wounded
The one who had been the warden of the treasures
For a long time, who had brought the terror of flame
Burning hot for the hoard, welling fiercely
In the middle of night, till he died a violent death.

The messenger was in haste, eager to return,
Impelled by the treasures; anxiety oppressed him—
Whether he, bold in spirit, would find the prince
Of the Weather-Geats drained out of strength still alive
In that place where earlier he had left him.
He then found the renowned prince, his lord
Besmeared in blood, along with the treasures,
At the end of his life. He again began to
Sprinkle water on him, till bits of words
Burst out through his breast. [The hero-king spoke,][104]
An old man in grief—casting his eyes on the gold—:
"I thank the Lord of all, the King of glory,
The eternal Lord, in my own words,
For the treasures that I gaze on here,

104. Klaeber supplemented within brackets the two words, "[Biorcyning spræc]," between "þurhbræc" (followed by a full stop) and "gomel"—the two words appearing with no intervening words in the MS. Wyatt and Chambers supplemented within brackets the two words, "[*Bīowulf reordode*,]." Dobbie's transcription shows three asterisks between "þurhbræc" (followed by a full stop) and "gomel." I follow Klaeber's textual emendation in my translation.

For my having been allowed to obtain such
For my people, before I breathe my last breath.
Now I have exhausted my life in old age
For the hoard of treasures, you further attend to
The need of my people; I cannot be here long.
Bid the battle-glorious men to build a burial mound,
A splendid one, after the pyre, on a sea promontory;
It is to tower high at the Whale's Headland,
As a memorial for my people,
So that the sea-faring men afterwards may call it
Beowulf's tomb—those who will sail ships across
The mist of the flooding waves from afar."
The brave-hearted prince took his golden ring
From his neck, and gave it to the thane,
To the young spear-warrior, and his gold-adorned helmet,
Bracelet and battle-gear, and bade him to use them well:
"You are the last one in our family line,
The Wægmundings; Fate has swept off all
My kinsmen to the decree of destiny,
All the earls valorous; I shall follow them."
That was for the old man the last word he uttered,
Coming from his heart, before he took to the pyre,
Hot and hostile flame; his soul departed from his heart
To seek the glory of the truth-bound ones.

[2821–3037: The runaways return to see Wiglaf tending on Beowulf dying; Wiglaf reproves the runaways; the herald reports the deaths of Beowulf and the dragon to the Geats; there follows a long digression on the feuds and the political entanglement that the Geats have had with their neighboring

nations, which ends with a pessimistic forecast of the fate of the Geats; the Geats go to the site of Beowulf's death.]

(XXXIX) Then it came to pass to the young man
With all the pain, that he on earth had to watch
His dearest lord at the end of his life
Go away pitiably. His slayer was also lying,
The dreadful earth-dragon deprived of life,
Overpowered by death. The twining serpent
Could not have control over the ring-hoard long,
For the swords' blades had taken him away,
The strong battle-sharp[105] leavings of hammers,
That the far-flier, quelled by his wounds,
Had fallen on the earth near the treasure.
Never again did he move about, flying in the air
At midnight, glorying in his precious properties,
And show his shape, for he had fallen on the earth,
Thanks to the feat the warlord's hands performed.
Indeed, according to what I have heard, no man
Of mighty achievements on earth, no matter how
Daring in all his deeds, did thrive in an attempt
To make a rush against the breath of the fatal foe
Or disrupt the hall of treasures with his hands,
If he discovered the keeper dwelling in the barrow
Wake up. A share of the lordly treasures came
To be Beowulf's, to be paid for only by his death:
Each had reached the end of his journey, as a part
Of the fleeting life. Then it was not long before
The wary watchers unfit for war left the wood,

105. "hearde heaðoscear*pe*" (Klaeber); "hearde, heaðoscearde" (Dobbie); "hearde, heaðo-scearde," (Wyatt and Chambers). Many editors follow Klaeber's reading, as I do.

The cowardly traitors, ten of them, all told,
Who had not dared before to fight with their spears
In the face of their liege lord's great need:
But they, feeling ashamed, bore their shields
And battle-garments to where the old man lay,
And they looked on Wiglaf. Wearied out, he was sitting,
A fighter on foot, near the shoulders of his lord;
He tried to awaken him with water—all to no avail.
He could not on earth, though he wished so much,
Keep hold of the strain of life in his liege lord,
Nor change anything already ordained by the Ruler:
God's decree would rule the deeds
For each of the men, as it now still does.

Then one who had lost courage earlier was
Bound to receive a grim answer from the young man.
Wiglaf spoke, son of Weohstan,
A grief-stricken man, looking on the unlovely ones:
"Alas, he who will speak truth can say that
Our liege lord, who gave you the rings,
The battle-gears that you there stand wearing,
When he at the ale-bench often bestowed on
Those sitting in the hall helmets and battle-shirts—
A prince to his thanes, such as he could find
Anywhere, far or near, the most splendid ones—
That he had utterly wasted all the battle-gear,
To his vexation, when war came upon him.
The people's king had no cause to boast of
His comrades in arms; however, God granted him,
The Ruler of victories did, to avenge himself alone
With his own sword, when his bravery was needed.

I could give him little aid at battle
To save his life, but nevertheless undertook to
Help my kinsman, though beyond my power.
When I struck the deadly foe with my sword,
He grew ever the weaker: the fire pouring out from
His head grew less powerful. Few of the defenders
Rushed to where the prince was, when hardship befell him.
Now treasure-receiving and sword giving,
Indeed all the home-joy and comfort, shall cease
For your people; each one of the men
Of your clan must move about deprived
Of land-right, when the noblemen happen to
Hear from afar of your flight, and of your
Inglorious behavior; for any man at arms,
Death is to be preferred over life in disgrace!"
(XL) Then he bade that the martial feat be announced
Within the walls, up over the sea-cliff, where the warriors
Sat in band, sad in heart, all the morning-tide,
Those shield-bearers, ready to hear one or the other—
That it was their dear lord's last day, or that
He was returning. He who rode up to the headland
Told new tidings without sparing his voice.
He truthfully said for all to hear:
"Now the giver of joy to the people of the Weathers,
The lord of the Geats, is fast bound to his death-bed;
He occupies a death-couch, quelled by the dragon.
Beside him lies his deadly opponent for life,
Stricken by dagger-wounds; he could not inflict
Any injury with his sword in any way
Upon the ferocious fiend. Wiglaf sits,

Son of Weohstan, and guards over Beowulf,
One warrior over another no longer alive;
Wearied in heart, he holds watch over the heads
Of his beloved and the loathed. Now the people
May look forward to a time of war, for the fall
Of our king will be widely known to the Franks
And to the Frisians. A fierce feud was fostered
Against the Hugas[106] when Hygelac went, faring
With his ship-borne force, to the land of the Frisians;
There the Hetware[107] made an assault on him in battle,
Swiftly brought it about with a stronger force
That the warrior[108] in battle-gear had to bow down,
And fell in the foot-band; the prince could not bestow
Treasures on his retainers.[109] Since that time
The Merovingian[110] has denied goodwill to us.[111]

"Nor do I expect from the people of Sweden
Either peace or good faith at all, for it's widely known
That Ongentheow deprived Hæthcyn,[112] son of Hrethel,
Of his life near the Wood of the Ravens, when
The people of the Geats, owing to their arrogance,
First made an assault on the War-Scylfings.

106. "The Hugas" is a name applied to the Franks.

107. "The Hetware" was a Frankish people on the lower Rhine.

108. "The warrior" refers to Hygelac.

109. It simply means that Hygelac, on account of his untimely death, did not even have a chance to reward his retainers after the battle.

110. "The Merovingian" refers to a king of the Franks.

111. Hygelac's raid on the Franks and the Frisians and his sub-sequent death in the battle have already been narrated earlier in the poem (ll. 1202–14a and ll. 2354b–66).

112. Hæthcyn, who succeeded Hrethel as king of the Geats, upon invading Swedish territory, was defeated and killed by Ongentheow. After his death, his brother Hygelac arrived with reinforcements, and made successful counter-attack on Ongentheow, who lost his life in the battle. Hygelac succeeded Hæthcyn as king of the Geats.

Soon the aged and wise father of Ohthere,[113]
Old and formidable, gave a counter-blow in return,
Cut down the sea-king,[114] rescued his wife,
An old woman of bygone days, deprived of gold,
Mother of Onela and of Ohthere;
And then he pursued his life-enemies
Till they escaped, barely saving their lives, to
The Holt of the Ravens, runaways deprived of their lord.
Then with his massive force he beset those still alive,
Weary with wounds; he often vowed woe
To the wretched band till dawn dispersed the dark:
He said he would in the morning crush them
With swords' edges, hang some on gallows
For the fowls to feast on. Comfort came again
To those sad in heart together with dawning,
When they heard Hygelac's horn and trumpet,
His sound, as the good man[115] came leading
A band of battle-ready men on the track they had left.
(XLI) The trail of blood of the Swedes and the Geats,
The murderous meeting of men was clearly visible—
How the peoples stirred up feud between them.
Then the good man[116] went with his kinsmen,
Silver-haired and sad, to seek his stronghold;
The earl Ongentheow moved higher up.
He had heard of the battle-force of Hygelac,
The proud man's power; he didn't count on counter-stroke,
Believe that he could withstand the seamen,

113. Ohthere and Onela were sons of Ongentheow.
114. "the sea-king" refers to Hæthcyn, then king of the Geats.
115. "the good man" refers to Hygelac.
116. "the good man" refers to Ongentheow.

Defend his hoard, children, and women against
The sailing fighters; the old man turned back from there
To hide behind an earth-wall. Pursuit was then
Pushed on to the people of the Swedes, the banners of
Hygelac swept forth over the stronghold for refuge, as
Hrethel's force[117] pressed forward to the fortress.
There Ongentheow, a gray-haired man,
Became driven to a halt at swords' edges,
That the people's king had to yield to the doom
Eofor alone assigned.[118] Wonred's son Wulf
Struck him with his weapon without restraint,
That blood spurted forth from veins after each stroke
To soak his hair. A Scylfing, though old, he was
Not afraid, nonetheless, but paid back quickly
With worse exchange for the deadly blow,
When, as king of a people, he turned thereto.
The brave son of Wonred[119] could not give
A return blow to the old man, for the latter
Had earlier cut through the helmet on his head,
That he had to bow down, besmeared in blood,
Fall on the earth; he[120] was not fated to die yet,
And he recovered, though his wound was deep.
The hardy thane of Hygelac,[121] when his brother fell,
Let his broad blade, the old sword forged by giants,
Break the helmet hardened by giants' hammers

117. "Hrethel's force" refers to the army led by Hygelac.

118. That is, Ongentheow's fate was in the hand of Eofor. Eofor and Wulf, Geatish warriors, were sons of Wonred. Hygelac made Eofor his son-in-law as a reward for slaying the Swedish king Ongentheow. (See ll. 2472-89 and ll. 2991-98.)

119. "son of Wonred" refers to Wulf.

120. That is, Wulf.

121. "the hardy thane of Hygelac" refers to Eofor.

Over the shield; then the king bowed down,
Protector of a people, having his life struck to the core.
Then there were many, who bound his brother's[122] wounds,
Raised him up rapidly, when it turned out that
They could now take charge of the battlefield.
Then the fighting man forfeited from the other,[123]
Stripped off Ongentheow his steel-woven gear,
His hard-hilted sword, and his helmet, as well;
He bore the battle-gear of the hoary man to Hygelac.
He took the treasure and solemnly promised him
Rewards among the people, and kept his word:
The lord of the Geats, son of Hrethel,
When he returned home, rewarded the battle-feat
Of Eofor and Wulf with sumptuous gifts,
And gave each of them a hundred-thousand [measurement]
Of land and linked rings—no cause to complain on the reward
For any man on the earth, for they had attained the glory by merit.
And then to Eofor he gave his only daughter,
As a pledge of good will—honor to any family.
That is the malevolence and the mutual malice,
The deadly hate between men, for which I expect
That the people of the Swedes will assault us,
When they learn that our lord is lifeless,
The man who has been a bulwark heretofore
Of our treasure and of our kingdom against enemies
After the fall of our heroes, the valiant shield-warriors,[124]
And performed for people's benefit till further yet he
Fulfilled heroic deeds. Now what is best for us is haste,.

122. That is, Wulf's

123. "the fighting man" refers to Eofor; "the other" refers to Ongentheow.

124 Here "the shield-warriors" are the Geats, not the Danes.

That we may look at the people's king there
And bring him, who has given us rings, on the way
To his funeral pyre. Nor is a little portion to melt
With the man of courage, but a mass of treasure is there,
Gold immeasurable, grimly gained,
And the rings bought now in the end
With his own life. Flame shall swallow these,
Fire enfold—never a man shall wear
A ring in remembrance, nor a fair maiden
Have round her neck a ring-adornment,
But shall, sad in heart, bereft of gold,
Tread on foreign land often, not just once,
Now our army-leader has laid aside his mirth,
Joy, and merriment. Therefore, many a spear,
Cold in the morning, shall be gripped in palms,
Heaved by hands; never the sound of the harp
Will waken up the warriors, but a dark raven,
Ready to devour the doomed, will croak loudly,
And report to the eagle how it has fared at the feast
While feeding upon the flesh with the wolf."

Thus the valiant man took the pain of telling
The grievous tidings, nor did he say much falsely about
What would happen or what had happened. The whole band arose;
They went, full of sorrow, under the Eagle's Bluff,[125]
To look on the wonder, with tears welling in their eyes.
Then they found him on the sand, soulless,
Reposing as if on a bed, who had given them rings
In bygone days; then the last day had come
For the brave man, that the battle-king,

125. "the Eagle's Bluff" ("Earna-næs") is a promontory in the land of the Geats, near which Beowulf fought the dragon.

Prince of the Weathers, died a wondrous death.

[3038–3182: The Geats prepare a funeral pyre, and mourn the death of their lord.]

First they beheld there the creature more than strange,
The serpent lying loathsome at the site, side by side,
Facing him there. It was the fire-dragon,
Terrifying in its varying colors, scorched by flame.
It was fifty-foot mark in full length as it lay
All stretched out; it had held the joy of
Flight in the air at night, was wont to go down to
Nestle in its den. Then it was held fast by death,
Had for the last time enjoyed its earth-caverns.
Beside it stood bowls and cups,
There lay plates and precious swords,
Eaten through by rust, the way they had remained
There in the earth's bosom for a thousand winters.
Then that heritage immensely huge, gold of
The men of old, had been wound up by spell,
That any of men would not be allowed to
Reach the ring-hall, unless God himself,
The Truly-victorious King, as men's protection,
Should grant him that He wished to open the hoard,
Even whoever of men as it seemed fit to Him.
(XLII) Then it was clear that the practice did not
Benefit him that had unjustly hidden the ornate works
Under the wall. The keeper at the outset had slain
One, of the few he killed. Then the hostile act came
To be severely punished. It is a wonder where

A warrior excelling in bravery should reach the end
Of life allotted to him, when he may no longer
Dwell in the mead-hall, a man with his kinsfolk.
So it was to Beowulf, when he sought strife with
The barrow's ward: he himself did not know
On what occasion his parting from the world should occur.
So the renowned princes, when they placed the treasure there,
Laid a deep curse on it to last till the day of doom—
That he who plunders the place, would be guilty of sins,
Confined in heathen temples, fixed with the bonds of hell,
And tormented grievously—
Unless he, desirous of the gold, had readily perceived
The good grace that the Owner had bestowed on him.[126]

Wiglaf spoke, son of Weohstan:
"Often due to one man's will many a man must
Endure misery, as it has happened to us.
We could not persuade our beloved prince,
Our kingdom's bulwark, by any counsel,
That he not attack the keeper of gold,
Let it lie where it had long been,
Remain at its dwelling-place till the world's end.
He held on to his high destiny. The hoard has been seen,
Grimly begotten; the fate was too powerful

126. Interpretation of the lines varies. One interpretation, to which I strongly object, is that made by Mitchell and Robinson, who explain the meaning of the lines: "Previously he [Beowulf] had not at all seen the gold-bestowing favour of God more clearly [i.e. God had never given Beowulf a greater treasure than this one]" (*Beowulf: An Edition*, 157, note). This is a wrong interpretation. What the lines emphasize is the time-honored doctrine that only those who are destined to receive God's special favor will come to possess the treasure; and, therefore, the injunction proclaimed by the princes who buried the treasure does not apply to one to whom God's grace has already been granted. This thought is in line with the Anglo-Saxons' attitude toward the issue of life and death in a battle: "Gæð a wyrd swa hio scel" (*Beowulf*, 454b).

That pushed the people's prince thereto.
I was in there and saw it all thoroughly,
The treasures in the hall, when I was granted access—
Far from being pleasant was the passage permitted
In under the earth-wall. In haste I grabbed
In my hands a massive mighty load of
Hoarded treasures, and took them out to here
To my king. He was then still alive,
His mind and senses all alert. He spoke many things,
Grand old man in grief, and bade me to greet you—
Ordered that you build at the site of the pyre
A mound mounting high in memory of your lord's deeds,
A monument big and well known, as he was of men
The worthiest warrior all throughout the world,
So long while he could enjoy the riches of his citadel.
Let us now hasten for a second time to
Visit and view the pile of the precious ornate gems,
A wonder under the walls; I will guide you,
That you may look on the rings and broad gold,
Plenty of them, right there. Let the palanquin be ready,
Prepared speedily, by the time we come out,
And then let us carry our lord,
Our beloved man, to where he shall long
Repose in the Ruler's protection."
Then the son of Weohstan, man brave in battle,
Bade to give orders to many of the warriors,
Of those who owned halls, that they, leaders of people,
Bring wood for the funeral pyre from far off,
For the brave man: "Now shall the fire swallow—
As flame grows dark—the chief of the warriors,

Who has lived through the shower of iron, when
The storm of arrows impelled by bowstrings
Swished over the shield-wall, shaft fulfilling its task,
Busy with its feather-gear, an aid to the arrowhead."
    Indeed, the wise son of Weohstan
Called forth from the troop thanes of the king,
Seven of them altogether, the very best of them.
One of the eight warriors, he went under
Their enemy's roof; one of them bore in his hand
A torch—he who walked ahead of the others.
Then who should plunder the hoard
Didn't need lot drawing, for men saw
Every part of it remain unwatched in the hall
And lie neglected. Little did any one grieve
That they had carried out in haste
The precious treasures. They also pushed the dragon,
The serpent, over the wall-cliff, let the wave take it,
Let the flood engulf the keeper of the fair treasures.
Then was loaded on a wagon the twisted gold,
Countless things of all sorts; and the prince,
The hoary warrior, was borne to the Whale's Headland.
(XLIII) Then the people of the Geats made ready
A funeral pyre for him, a splendid one on the earth,
Hung round with helmets, battle-shields,
Bright battle-shirts, as he had bidden.
Then they laid down in the middle their renowned prince,
Their beloved lord; the men did so, mourning.
Then the warriors began to kindle on the hill
The greatest of funeral fires. Wood-smoke arose,
Black over the fire; the roaring flame bellowed,

Mingling with the weeping—the twirling wind died out—
Till it had burnt down the bone-wrapping body-flesh,
Hot in its heart. With their souls soaked in sadness,
They mourned the death of their lord, deep in their hearts.
So, grief-stricken, an old Geatish woman sang
A mournful song after Beowulf, with her tangled
Hair bound up, and said over and over again
That she dreaded the evil days ahead sorely,
Plenty of slaughters, terror of the invading troop, being
Demeaned and enslaved. Heaven swallowed the smoke.
　　Then the people of the Weather-Geats built
A mound on the headland, which was high and broad,
To be seen by the seafarers far and wide;
And they built in ten days a monument to
The battle-brave one, and surrounded the ashes
With a wall, the way the men most prudent
Would find it to be in a way most worthy.
They placed in the barrow rings and jewels,
All such ornaments as from the hoard before
The men who were hostile-minded had taken.
They let the earth hold the wealth of warriors,
Gold in the earth, where it now still stays,
As useless to men, the way it was before.
　　Then the battle-brave ones rode round the mound—
Inheritors of noble blood, twelve all told—
Uttering words of grief over loss of their lord
In a mournful dirge to commemorate their king.
They lauded his manliness, and spoke highly of
His brave deeds—as it befits a man
To praise his dear lord in words,

While longing springs in his heart, when he
Is finally freed from the confinement of flesh.
So the people of Geatland mourned the death
Of their lord, recalling the warmth of his hearth.
They said that, of all earthly kings, he was
The gentlest of men, the most warm-hearted,
Kindest to his people, and most eager for fame.

Genealogical Charts

The Danes, or the Scyldings:

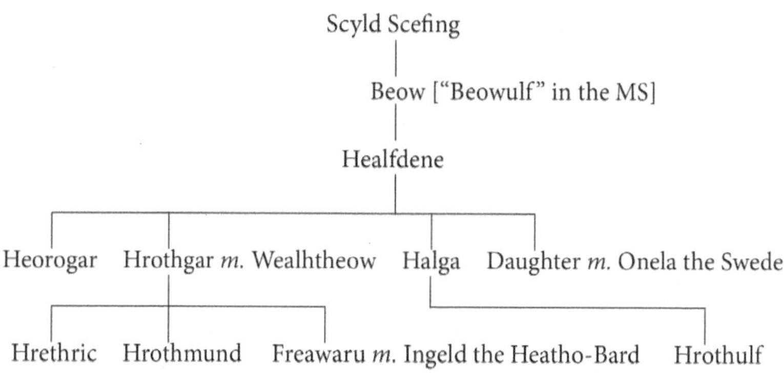

The Geats:

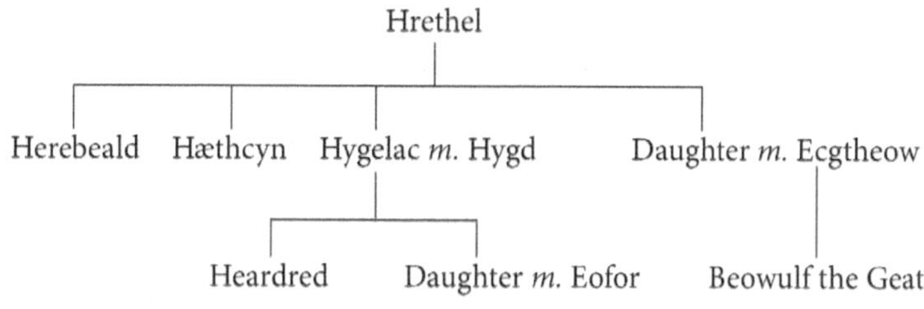

The Swedes:

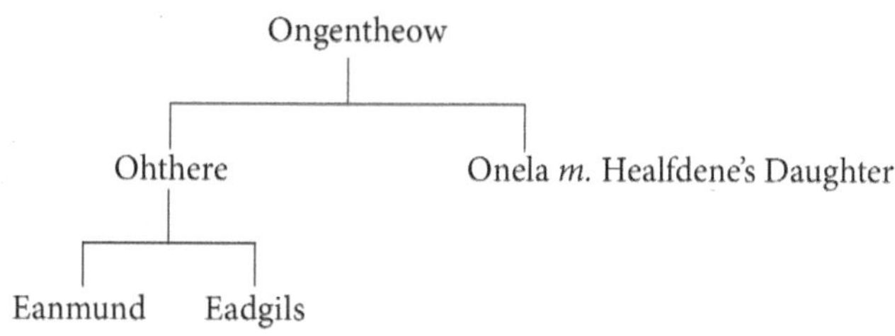

Appendix

The Digressions in *Beowulf*

A reader of *Beowulf* finds it puzzling that the narrator occasionally shifts to an apparently extraneous episode that does not seem to bear much relevance to the main narrative in progress. It is an extra burden for the reader. One might ascribe it to literary convention, for interpolating digressions was a common practice in the composition of an epic. Compliance with literary convention, however, has to be justified by its contribution in intensifying the auditor's (or the reader's) absorption in the world of poetic imagination that evolves in an epic. The unexpected intrusion of passages that seem to have no direct relevance to the progress of the main narrative is thus bound to puzzle the reader, and may lead one to wonder whether it was really necessary for the poet to switch to a long digression at any given moment.

There are several digressions in *Beowulf*; and to argue that they indeed fit into the making of the poem is my task now—which is none other than trying to prove the validity of their presence. While translating *Beowulf*, I occasionally felt somewhat irritated whenever the progress of the main narrative was interrupted by the sudden switch to an apparently extraneous episode. Convincing the readers of *Beowulf* that these digressions are not irrelevant to the continuity of its epic narration, therefore, is what I undertake now. Unless each instance of digression proves to be a part contributing to effective buildup of the epic saga of Beowulf, one might conclude that, after all, it was a mere addition having no relevance to the progress of the main narrative.

To jump to my conclusion: I wish to assert that the digressions in *Beowulf* are important segments of the poem, which enhance its epic flow. To take a digression simply as manifestation of literary convention, or to regard it as mere addition, is doing injustice to this particular aspect in the artistry of *Beowulf*. By calling the reader's attention to how each digression does indeed fit into the progress of the narrative, I wish to demonstrate that it is not a redundant part we may as well do without, but an element that enriches the poem.

The first digression to appear in the poem (874b–915) is about the life-story of Sigemund, a hero in the Northern saga, and that of Heremod, a Danish king in the remote past. The two characters are mentioned, respectively representing success and failure, each as the ruler of a nation. This digression occurs in that part of the poem telling the festive occasion of celebrating Beowulf's victory over Grendel. A thane of Hrothgar, while entertaining the Danes and the Geats elated by Beowulf's triumphant success in vanquishing Grendel, recites the life-stories of Sigemund and Heremod—which do not seem to have any direct relevance to that occasion. How should we interpret the poet's intention in inserting these forty-some lines, which momentarily divert the auditor's attention to what lies outside the mainstream of the narrative?

The thane who was "endowed with eloquence . . . devised another tale with well-woven words: he in turn started to sing of the feat of Beowulf . . . and composed a tale successfully with his skills, with words set anew" (869–75a). Then the digression on the lives of Sigemund and Heremod follows. How should we relate the glory of Beowulf with the grandeur of Sigemund's life and the misery of Heremod's? The poet's intention is clear: it is to measure Beowulf's future life up against the two contrasting life-stories of Sigemund and Heremod. Heremod is mentioned again later in the poem, in Hrothgar's speech to Beowulf (1709b–22a), in which the former gives advice on becoming a successful ruler. What strikes the reader as somewhat significant in this digression is Sigemund's slaying the dragon guarding a treasure-hoard. It surely foreshadows, in retrospect, Beowulf's slaying the fire-spewing dragon toward the end of the poem. Perhaps the poet subconsciously wanted to make Beowulf's eventual death more poignant by telling the auditors of Sigemund's triumphant return with the hoard after slaying its warden.

It is quite possible that the poet inserted this digression (874b–915) and the passage (867b–74a) introducing it later, for if we skip the whole part (867b–915), the flow of the lines becomes smoother and it makes more sense in terms of the sequence of the events:

> Now and again the battle-brave ones let their bay steeds
> Gallop and run to compete with one another,
> Where the foot-paths looked fair, not falling short of
> Their fame as fine tracks. (864–67a) [Skip 867b–915]
> At times, competing on horseback, they raced
> On the sandy roads, when the morning light
> Had approached and hastened. Many a retainer,
> Firmly resolved, went to the high hall
> To see the strange wonder; the king himself,
> The guardian of the treasure-hoards with fame for virtues,
> Also carried his steps in triumph from his conjugal quarter,
> Attended by a large retinue; and his queen with him,
> Followed by a train of waiting ladies, trod the path to the mead-hall.
> (916–24)

The thanes ride their horses in jubilee to Heorot to celebrate Beowulf's victory: that is the overall picture we get from reading these lines. Moreover, the poetically endowed thane's recitation of a song extolling Beowulf's feat, and of other old tales, had to occur in Heorot—not during their horse riding. In the extant manuscript, Hrothgar's commendatory speech on Beowulf's feat, and the latter's unvarnished report to the former on how he overcame Grendel, appear *after* the digression in question. It is logically appropriate, however, for any entertainment (such as a thane's recitation of old tales) to follow this formal exchange of words. For these obvious reasons, I suspect that the poet added the Sigemund-Heremod digression later, with the result that it causes confusion in the sequence of the events. Clearly, this digression was not part of the text the poet had initially composed, but a later addition.

The second digression (1068–1159a) is the recounting of a feud between the Danes and the Jutes, which is made here in a highly allusive manner, so much so that we need the supplementation of an Old English poetic fragment, The Fight at Finnsburg, to have a grasp of the storyline. Setting forth the story in detail may not be necessary here. Let it suffice to call to mind the backbone of the story—a friendly visit made in all good intention ending with a disastrous and tragic outcome:

> Hnæf the Dane pays a visit to his sister Hildeburh, queen of Finn the Jute. Quite unexpectedly, a fray breaks out between the Danes and the Jutes, and Hnæf and Finn's son are killed in the scuffle; thus Hideburh loses both her brother and her son. Her tragedy does not end there: her husband Finn also gets killed in time by Hnæf's thane Hengest, who, after temporary and precarious reconciliation with the Jutes, avenges his lord's death, and she herself is taken to the land of her birth as a captive on the Danes' journey back home.

The digression occurs in the middle of the passages depicting the banquet held to celebrate Beowulf's victory over Grendel. On this festive occasion, why the recitation of a gruesome tale of bloodshed between kinsfolk and breakup of a tie between two nations attained by marriage? When the digression is over, there follows Wealhtheow's addressing Hrothgar and Beowulf. In her wish-making speech to her husband (1169–87) she stresses her belief in a good bond between their sons and their nephew Hrothulf, son of Halga, in the future. And in her words of compliment to Beowulf (1216–31) she requests him to be a guardian for her sons. A few lines that precede her address to Hrothgar sound suggestive:

> Then forth came Wealhtheow,
> Wearing a golden diadem, to where the brave twain
> Sat, nephew and uncle; then their friendship was still fair,
> Each true to the other. (1162b–65a)

The implication is that Hrothulf, though apparently on good terms with his uncle Hrothgar now, may turn out disloyal to him. When Wealhtheow specifically mentions the love and care bestowed on Hrothulf by her and her husband, somehow it may be an indication of her concern about the possibility of Hrothulf becoming a threat to the Danish throne in time. A woman's premonition of what will happen later? It may be so. But, to get back to the question of the interpolation of the digression: the tragic outcome of Hnæf's visiting his sister Hildeburh (which he did in nothing but good intention) is proof enough that the present circumstance is no guarantee of a good turnout in the future. Thus, the digression fits into the context of the evolution of the narrative, foreshadowing Hrothulf's potential treachery, despite his present affability.

While the ring-giving to Beowulf goes on, the narrator inserts some lines (1197–1214a) that relate the transmission—which has happened before and will happen afterwards—of the precious items he receives. What is said in these eighteen lines sounds rather cryptic, but it certainly makes it clear that any treasure given to a man cannot remain his for long: the treasure exists by itself, and owning it does not mean that it belongs to its owner—for any precious item, on account of its rarity, is bound to move from hand to hand as time passes. The transitoriness of the glory of owning a treasure looms here as a thought that prevails the whole epic. Even the dragon's hoard that Beowulf comes to seize at the cost of his life cannot be his, or even the Geats': it all has to be buried along with his ashes, as being useless for men. What "the last survivor" utters (2247–66) reinforces the idea of the futility of attaching any meaning to owning a treasure. Thus, the cryptic words on the transmission—before and after—of the gifts bestowed on Beowulf take on a meaning not to be overlooked: the transience of all worldly possession or glory.

The futility of men's wish for retaining what they "own," or attaining a goal through arbitrary transaction, is repeatedly emphasized throughout the poem. Effort to rebuild good relation by creating marriage-ties between tribes or nations, for instance, will turn out futile. That is what Beowulf tells Hygelac in his report on his sojourn at Heorot (2020–69a). He predicts that Hrothgar's attempt to secure peace with Ingeld the Heatho-Bard, his hostile neighbor, by marrying off his daughter Freawaru to him, will be futile: Freawaru will not become a successful peace-weaver, as Hrothgar expects—not because of her inadequacy as a bride, but because of the inveterate hostilities in the Heatho-Bards. Though this is part of Beowulf's speech to Hygelac, it can very well be read as a digression revealing the poet's own thought on the inevitability of what *wyrd* dictates in the evolution of human affairs.

When the narration reaches the point where Beowulf, as old king of the Geats, prepares himself for his fight with the dragon, the narrator provides a retrospective account of the battles he has gone through. In this digression (2354b–96), the narrator tells the auditors a sequence of the past events that have occurred from the time when he was a loyal thane of Hygelac till he proved himself a most competent king—meting justice, even beyond his domain:

> Lines 2354b–79a: Beowulf fought in the battle against the Frisians, in which Hygelac died, and Wealhtheow's gift to Beowulf, which Hygelac was wearing, fell into the hands of the Franks. When Beowulf returned home lordless, having performed not a small martial feat in the war, Hygelac's queen Hygd asked Beowulf to take over the rule of the nation, for she didn't think her son Heardred was ready to inherit the throne; but Beowulf declined the queen's offer, and remained loyal to the young prince as his guardian till the latter grew into maturity.

The ensuing part of the digression tells us of the occasion of Heardred's death and of Beowulf's revenge of his death:

> Lines 2379b–96: When Eanmund and Eadgils, Ohthere's two sons, sought refuge at Heardred's court, fleeing from their uncle Onela, who had usurped the Swedish throne after his brother Ohthere's death, the Geats protected them well. In revenge for the favor that Heardred extended to Eanmund and Eadgils, Onela attacked the Geats, and in the battle Heardred and Eanmund died. Content with the deaths of the two men, Onela returned to Sweden, thus leaving the Geats without a ruler. Beowulf ascended the throne, took good care of Eadgils, and eventually helped the latter seize the Swedish throne after slaying Onela in revenge for the deaths of Heardred and Eanmund.

The above digression not only fits well into the progress of the narrative, but also provides strong momentum for the auditors to envision Beowulf's final fight with the dragon, in which he is to reach the end of his life. Moreover, the story of the feud between the Geats and the Swedes introduced here is carried over in other passages interpolated sparsely while the main narrative goes on, with the result that the auditors get the feeling that the intermittently appearing digressions on the feud constitute a storyline on its own, quite independent of the story of Beowulf's life—like a separate tune heard along with the main tune, creating beautiful harmony while the two crisscross each other.

In his recollection of his youthful days, Beowulf, who feels that the impending fight with the dragon will be his last battle, recounts the pain and sorrow of Hrethel over his eldest son Herebeald's accidental death from his second son Hæthcyn's bungling. According to the old law of vendetta, Hæthcyn should have been hanged for killing Hrethel's would-be heir, Herebeald; but Hrethel could not deprive another son of his life. Hrethel pined away, finally to lie on his deathbed (2435–71). What relevance does this "digression" have to the main narrative? Later, when Beowulf utters his dying words to Wiglaf, he regrets having no fleshly heir to inherit his battle-gear; but he bequeaths it to Wiglaf, the last of the Wægmundings, of which he is one. When Hrethel's grief over having lost his would-be heir Herebeald is put side by side with the absolute loneliness that Beowulf has to embrace as he encounters the dragon all by himself, the implication of the digression is clear: Beowulf stays far above the realm of the common worldlings, who attach much meaning to their fleshly ties. Nowhere in the poem do we find any mention of his conjugal life, which means that he was not meant to leave any offspring behind to succeed him, to carry on his bloodline. Beowulf's spiritual son Wiglaf would have said, "Take him for all in all, you shall not look upon his like again." Beowulf was not meant to have a biological heir; only the monument raised on the promontory to be seen from afar by the seafaring men was to make them recall that there once was a king of the Geats named Beowulf.

Having mentioned Hrethel's death, Beowulf (or, more accurately, the narrator, who is merely borrowing Beowulf's mouth in the ensuing part of the digression) tells how Hæthcyn, who succeeded Hrethel, died in a war against the Swedes (2472–83), and how Hygelac, who succeeded Hæthcyn, avenged his brother Hæthcyn's death by having Ongentheow the Swede slain in battle (2484–89). Hygelac's death in battle was mentioned earlier in the poem (2354b–79a), but in that preceding passage the narrator did not say anything about Beowulf's avenging his lord's death before returning home. Here we hear directly from Beowulf that his "fierce handgrip crushed [Dæghrefn's] pulsating heart—the flesh covering his bones" (2507–8), in revenge for his having slain Hygelac.

Why all this recounting of the deaths of the foregoing kings of the Geats? Earlier in the poem (2354b–96) the narrator told us how Beowulf declined Hygd's offer of the Geatish throne after her husband Hygelac's death, how he acted as a protégé for Hygelac's son Heardred till the latter grew into maturity, and also how he meted justice, after Heardred's death, even beyond the sea, by reinstating Eadgils as the legitimate heir of the Swedish throne. So far, all his life, Beowulf has been a bulwark of the Geats, both as a loyal thane and as a king. Now the time has come for him to conclude his life in a fight he must carry on in order to save his people. The recounting of the foregoing Geatish kings' deaths, and of what Beowulf has done so far, either as a thane or as a ruling monarch, prepares the auditors to hear his last pledge to confront the dragon all alone. Beowulf's resolution to face the dragon all by himself should not be taken as an indication of his hubris or megalomania: he knows that he will die in that battle, and also that he will somehow put an end to the devastation perpetrated by the dragon. A king caring for his hearth-companions, Beowulf does not want them to be exposed to the danger of physical harm, which they certainly will receive when they accompany him in the fight. In that sense, Beowulf, at this point of the narration, is a magnificent martyr-figure—the way Christ was.

The last digression in *Beowulf* appears in the herald's report to the Geats of Beowulf's demise and the dragon's death, toward the very end of the poem (2910b–3007a). It is about the feuds and the political entanglement that the Geats have had with their neighboring nations, and it ends with a pessimistic forecast of the fate of the Geats, now that Beowulf is gone. The long retrospective recounting of the feuds between the Geats and their neighboring nations—the Franks, the Frisians, and the Swedes—, in which the deaths of Hygelac and Ongentheow are mentioned, indeed sounds inappropriate to be part of the herald's message announcing Beowulf's death to the Geats. The whole digression reads like a later addition, rather than an outcome of the natural flow of verse-making. As a matter of fact, the herald's message would have more urgency and would be more moving, without this long recounting of the past events. If we skip the "digression" (2910b–3007a) as we read, the herald's speech sounds more natural. This digression, or insertion of the past history, slackens the urgency of the herald's message, to be felt as we envision the Geats listening to the heartbreaking news of their lord's demise.

Then why does the last digression appear, which only blunts the edge of the immediate poignancy of Beowulf's death? The herald, a learned historian that he is—in view of his detailed recounting of the past history—simply does not sound like a mere bringer of the sad news of Beowulf's death while the digression continues. Surely, this last digression to appear in *Beowulf* could not have been part of the text the poet had initially composed. One might even venture to surmise that, as the poet wished to cast a bleak shadow of doom over the future fate of the Geats deprived of the protection of Beowulf as their guardian, he might have felt the urge to add this digression later, which feelingly asserts the inevitability of the impending national disaster.

So far, I have tried to re-read the "digressions" in *Beowulf* in hopes of embracing them as an integral part of the poem, which only enriches it at the cost of occasionally bewildering the auditors by their unexpected appearance in the course of the narrative. Whether they were a natural outgrowth of the verse-making the *Beowulf*-poet was engaged in while composing the poem, or later additions, is a question that cannot be answered with any certainty by posterity. These digressions should be taken as evidence of the poetic flourishes a creative artist wished to demonstrate as part of his mastery in the art of verse-making. Sometimes the digressions help to elevate the tenor of *Beowulf* as an epic; sometimes their presence leads the flow of the narrative into momentary bathos. We must remember, however, that in a work of art of grand scale, whether a landscape drawing for sweeping vision or a grand symphony encompassing the whole diapason of powerful notes, we see or hear the parts integral to its makeup, while certain parts look or sound not so much so, or occasionally out of the way, or overdone. Hence, each time the readers encounter a digression in *Beowulf*, it is up to them to decide which case it is.

Bibliography

Dobbie, Elliott Van Kirk, ed. *The Anglo-Saxon Minor Poems.* The Anglo-Saxon Poetic Records, Vol. VI. New York: Columbia University Press, 1942.

———, ed. *Beowulf and Judith.* The Anglo-Saxon Poetic Records, Vol. IV. New York: Columbia University Press, 1953.

Donaldson, E. Talbot, tr. *Beowulf: A New Prose Translation.* London: Norton, 1966.

Jack, George, ed. *Beowulf: A Student Edition.* Oxford: Oxford University Press, 1995.

Klaeber, Fr., ed. *Beowulf and the Fight at Finnsburg.* 3rd ed. Lexington, MA: Heath, 1950; 4th ed. Re-edited by R. D. Fulk, Robert E. Bjork, and John D. Niles. Toronto: University of Toronto Press, 2008.

Krapp, George Philip, and Elliott Van Kirk Dobbie, eds. *The Exeter Book.* The Anglo-Saxon Poetic Records, Vol. III. New York: Columbia University Press, 1936.

Lee, Sung-Il, tr. *Beowulf in Parallel Texts.* Eugene, OR: Cascade Books, 2017.

Mitchell, Bruce, and Fred C. Robinson, eds. *Beowulf: An Edition with Relevant Shorter Texts.* Oxford: Blackwell, 2006.

Morgan, Edwin, tr. *Beowulf: A Verse Translation into Modern English.* Berkeley: University of California Press, 1952.

Wyatt, A. J., ed. *Beowulf with the Finnsburg Fragment.* New edition revised with Introduction and Notes by R. W. Chambers. Cambridge: Cambridge University Press, 1920.

Zupitza, Julius, ed. *Beowulf: Reproduced in Facsimile from the Unique Manuscript, British Museum MS. Cotton Vitellius A. XV with a Transliteration and Notes.* 2nd ed. Introduction and Notes by Norman Davis. Oxford: Oxford University Press, 1959.

About the Translator

Sung-Il Lee, born in 1943, studied English literature at Yonsei University (BA, 1967), the University of California, Davis (MA, 1973), and Texas Tech University (PhD, 1980). He taught at Yonsei University from 1981 until he retired in 2009. While he was on leave of absence, he taught as a visiting professor at the University of Toronto (1987), the University of Washington (1994–95), and Troy State University (2002–3). He was one of the founding members of the Medieval English Studies Association of Korea (now the Medieval and Early Modern English Studies Association of Korea), and served as its president for 1996–98. He is now Professor Emeritus at Yonsei University.

His major publications in the field of Old English poetry include *Beowulf in Parallel Texts* (Cascade, 2017) and *Twelve Old English Poems* (Resource Publications, 2025). He has also translated Korean poetry, both modern and classical, into English, and has published a total of fifteen anthologies, including *The Wind and the Waves: Four Modern Korean Poets* (1989), for which he received the Grand Prize in The Republic of Korea Literary Award in 1990, *The Moonlit Pond: Korean Classical Poems in Chinese* (1998), which was listed as an Outstanding Academic Book of 1998 by *Choice*. His ongoing publication of Korean translations of Shakespearean and non-Shakespearean drama includes *Richard II* (2011), *Julius Caesar* (2011), *Richard III* (2012), *Othello* (2013), *Macbeth* (2014), *The Duchess of Malfi* (2012), and *Dr. Faustus* (2014). Twice a prize-winner in *The Korea Times* Modern Korean Literature Translation Contest, he received the Grand Prize in translation in the Republic of Korea Literary Awards (1990) and the Fourth Biennial Korean Literature Translation Award (1999), both given by the Korean Culture and Arts Foundation.

www.ingramcontent.com/pod-product-compliance
Lightning Source LLC
LaVergne TN
LVHW090523110826
845146LV00003B/962